'For goodness' sake!'

The deep voice was crisp with exasperation again. 'I'm perfectly respectable. I have a mother who dotes on me, no brothers or sisters unfortunately, but stacks of cousins and an aunt who thinks I'm perfect. Besides all that I'm a doctor. Now, do you want me to take you to the city or will you come with me through to Toowoomba?'

A doctor! To end up in a stranger's car, and find out he was a doctor . . .

Dear Reader

Although our heroines have quite serious problems this month, we accentuate the positive, and show that even in the darkest hours we should not lose hope that there will be light at the end of the tunnel. And Christmas is coming—how could we be sad about that? Stay cheerful!

The Editor

!!!STOP PRESS!!! If you enjoy reading these medical books, have you ever thought of writing one? We are always looking for new writers for LOVE ON CALL, and want to hear from you. Send for the guidelines, with SAE, and start writing!

Mary Hawkins lives with her minister husband and two of their three grown children in the Hunter Valley north of Sydney, but still thinks of herself as a Queenslander! She is a registered nurse who returned to her profession several years ago after a long break and found tremendous changes in the medical world. Now her love of nursing has been surpassed by her love of writing, but close contacts in the medical profession help keep her stories current and real to life.

Recent titles by the same author:

ONGOING CARE
PRIORITY CARE

BURNOUT

BY

MARY HAWKINS

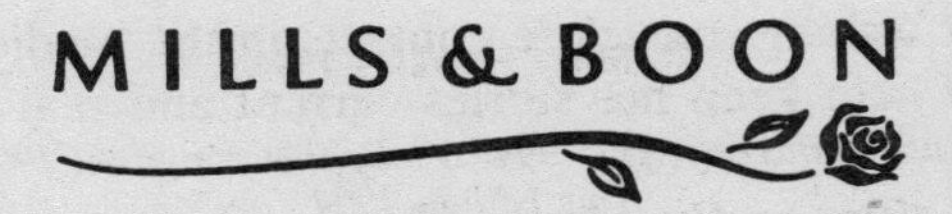

MILLS & BOON LIMITED
ETON HOUSE, 18-24 PARADISE ROAD
RICHMOND, SURREY TW9 1SR

First published in Great Britain 1994
by Mills & Boon Limited

This edition 1994

ISBN 0 263 78856 3

Set in Times 10 on 11½ pt.

03-9411-47435

Made and printed in Great Britain

CHAPTER ONE

THE suitcases moving past Jodi on the conveyor belt seemed suddenly to go on forever, and still her own battered one covered in various foreign countrys' stickers had not come through from those mysterious regions every airport seemed to possess. She slung her heavy handbag to her other shoulder, sighed, and rubbed the back of her neck where the persistent ache was getting worse.

Suddenly she felt her body sway and closed her eyes tightly.

'Are you OK?'

The hand grasping her elbow firmly steadied her, and the deep masculine voice beside her sounded concerned.

'Mmm. . .nothing a good sleep wouldn't cure,' she murmured, not quite truthfully, as she turned carefully with a forced smile.

And then was still.

It was the man who had sat across the aisle from her on the flight from Sydney to Brisbane. She had noticed him watching her several times, and each time he had seemed to frown at her when she caught his eye. Once she had been sure he was going to speak to her, and for some inexplicable reason she had turned swiftly away and pretended to be dozing. The very last thing she needed was for a strong-jawed, tall, dark and handsome hunk to try to strike up a conversation when she felt so filthy and exhausted.

But she had been unable to do more than doze very lightly. Her mind was still too filled with the sights, smells and trauma of the past six months, culminating in these last few dreadful weeks. There had been very little real sleep for so long that she had felt she dared not relax her guard. Not yet. Soon, very soon now. But not yet. . .

Perhaps when her brother arrived. Perhaps when he came and whisked her away to the peace he had promised her in his last letter. It had arrived so unexpectedly in the mail after a particularly fraught day. With the sweat on her face mingling with her tears as she had clutched his precious letter, she had suddenly longed to get to know him properly, and his beloved Ann and their little daughter. Most of all, she had longed to be away from the never-ending stream of sick and dying people. . .away from. . .

'Look, give me your baggage number, describe your case, and go and sit down while I wait for it.'

Perhaps if that deep baritone had not sounded quite so impatient, or certainly not as bossy, Jodi would have agreed immediately. But it seemed as if for days now she had been surrounded by bossy people arranging her life for her without any reference to her own hard-earned independence or even her wishes.

'No, thank you,' she managed to say politely, 'I can manage.'

'But you look as though a puff of wind would blow you away, and you're so pale——'

'I said I can manage!' She heard the sudden shrillness in her voice as she yanked her arm away from the warmth of his hand.

Thankfully she spotted the distinctive dark red suitcase coming towards her at last, and moved abruptly to claim it. But a lean, tanned hand was there before her.

'This one yours?' There was a hint of amusement in the man's voice now. 'Good grief! It weighs a ton! Must have cost a fortune in excess weight. Whatever do you have in it?'

'Give it to me, please.'

Her voice was now very controlled, but carried the whiplash that had made many a misbehaving patient think twice before defying Sister Banner.

This man just grinned at her. 'No, I'll carry it for you until you at least get a trolley. Are you being met?'

It suddenly took every ounce of effort Jodi could dredge up not to scream at him. This domineering, confident, macho type of man was the kind she detested the most!

Biting her bottom lip, she glared at him, for a moment frightened that she would really lose the last remnant of the self-control she had been holding on to desperately for what now seemed like aeons.

'Give me my case!'

He quirked a thick eyebrow and waited.

'Yes, I am being met,' she spat at him through clenched teeth, 'and if you don't let go of my belongings immediately I'm going to start the biggest ruckus this arrival area has ever seen!'

His expression changed. The case was thumped down on the carpet. 'Don't think it's your charming manner, young lady, that drew me to offer my assistance! And even if you were the most glamorous woman in the world, instead of freckled, red-haired, bad-tempered. . .it wouldn't matter a. . .a. . .I'm off all females at the moment!'

Dark eyes glared at her. 'And I'd have to be darned hard up to try and crack on to a sickly, anorexic piece of womanhood like you. But the air hostess was worried and asked me to keep an eye on you. Apparently you were staggering up the departure corridor at Sydney. So, if you're sure you're not going to be sick any moment or keel over, I'll be on my way!' He glared arrogantly at her for a moment longer, and then she was watching his broad back moving rapidly away from her.

Freckled, red-haired, anorexic! She shuddered. At least he had not said a nervous wreck! Then regret lashed through her. After all, he had only been trying to help. There was no need for her to have been so . . . so dreadfully rude!

Her body began to tremble again as it had when she had hurried from the international terminal at Mascot to just make it on to the Brisbane flight. There had been only a slight delay getting through Customs, but that last-minute rush had nearly finished her.

Jodi glanced desperately around. The flight had arrived a few minutes late and there had been considerable delay in unloading the plane. She checked her watch and knew her brother should have been here to meet her by this time if he was coming at all. Mail services had been erratic from the bush village, and she had tried unsuccessfully to phone him after reaching a more civilised area. But surely her cable from Nairobi would have arrived in plenty of time?

Perhaps Jimmy had not wanted her despite his wonderful letter telling her how pleased he had been that she had written, and asking her to visit them when she had finished her stint in Africa.

She pushed that dreadful thought aside but her trembling increased. How would she get to Toowoomba if no one met her? And the farm was still further west, altogether well over two hours from here by car, he had told her.

That handsome stranger had been right, cruelly so. She was almost at the end of her strength.

She hesitated for a moment, and then, cursing herself for being a fool, she dragged her case on its small castors over to the nearest phone booth. Wearily clutching the handpiece, she listened to the phone ringing uselessly at her brother's home.

'Sorry, madam, the airport bus to the city transport terminal departed only a couple of minutes ago. You'll have to wait for the next,' she was told abruptly at the enquiry counter a few moments later.

She collapsed on to a chair and opened her purse to check how much cash she had left for a taxi, when she was suddenly aware that a pair of dark-clad legs had come to stand close beside her.

'Oh, Jimmy——' she began with delight as she looked up, only to break off and stare at the scowling face above her.

'So, the boyfriend has stood you up, after all. Just as well I came back. Now, will you accept some help or not?'

'I. . . I. . .'

'Look! My car's parked quite illegally just outside, so make up your mind fast!'

Jodi just stared at him. He gave an impatient shrug, and started to turn away. She sprang to her feet, and a wave of exhaustion swept through her again.

'Wait!' she called out in a shaky voice 'Are. . .are you going into the city?'

'I can.'

She took a deep breath. 'Then thank you, yes, please, I would like a lift.'

His face relaxed slightly. He reached over and grabbed her case again, and without a word took off rapidly towards the large glass exit doors.

Was she an absolute fool? she thought in trepidation as she started after him. She was about to accept a ride in a total stranger's car as countless mothers had warned countless daughters never to do!

But the danger was negligible in comparison to that nerve-racking fear that had been her companion for the last few weeks, she thought grimly.

By the time she had caught up with him, he was already lifting the heavy case effortlessly into the boot of a car. And it wasn't just any old car. Jodi's eyes recognised the logo on the smooth curve of the bonnet. A gleaming white Mercedes Benz, no less! And as late a model by the shape of its modern lines as her father's black one! Who was this bossy man?

There was a loud blast of a horn as Jodi hesitated, and then the man was beside her.

'Get in,' he said curtly as he swung open the car door.

The irate taxi driver leaned on his horn again. A soft rain was falling and his cab was holding up several cars while he was waiting to claim his parking area. Jodi felt the grip of the stranger again, and then found herself bundled into the front passenger seat. Before she could catch her breath, the car was pulling away to the accompaniment of a couple of derisive horn blasts.

'Well, now, perhaps it's time we exchanged names.' His manner was still abrupt.

Jodi was fumbling with her seatbelt, and as it clicked into place she said shortly, 'Jodi Banner.'

'Scott Campbell. And whereabouts in the city do you want to be dropped off?'

Jodi hesitated and turned towards him. He was still concentrating on negotiating the traffic as they neared the airport exit. 'I. . .I don't want to take you out of your way. Where. . .where are you making for?'

He turned and his sudden smile transformed his dark features. 'Actually, I'm going to get out of this city as quickly as I can. After Sydney, it'll be wonderful to be back in the bush away from exhaust fumes, traffic lights and hordes of people rushing everywhere! I'm going west to Toowoomba and beyond, but I can——'

'Toowoomba! But that's where I was going to get a coach to.'

'That's solved that, then. We'll turn here.' He swerved the car into the other lane. 'I'd much rather negotiate the outskirts than get tangled up in the inner-city traffic, especially with this drizzly rain.'

For one panicky moment, Jodi felt as though her life was out of her control and in the hands of a stranger—once again. 'But. . .but I'm not sure. . .'

'For goodness' sake!' The deep voice was crisp with exasperation again. 'I'm perfectly respectable. I have a mother who dotes on me, no brothers or sisters unfortunately, but stacks of cousins, an aunt who thinks I'm perfect and a minister of religion who can vouch that I attend church as regularly as my work permits, and who would applaud my efforts to be a Good Samaritan! And besides all that I'm a doctor. Now, do you want me to take you to the city or will you come with me through to Toowoomba?'

A doctor! It was just typical of her life these past weeks! To end up in a stranger's car, and find out he was a doctor, when the very last thing she wanted even to think about was the medical profession, and patients, and illness, and death, and. . .

Jodi's head was throbbing now. Holding her hands tightly together to try and stop them shaking, she sat rigidly, fighting to maintain what little control she had left.

'Please,' she managed in a trembling voice, 'I'm sorry. I've been ill and am still suffering from jet-lag. I'm very grateful. Toowoomba would be fine.'

She was aware the man had glanced sharply across at her as she began to talk, but she stared miserably straight ahead through the windscreen.

'Well, if you've been ill, you'd probably prefer to relax for a while instead of talking,' Scott's voice drawled softly. And then she thought she heard him mutter, 'Even though I'd sure like to know what's up with you.'

In some part of her brain, Jodi knew she should be alarmed. But as she closed her eyes and rested her head back, a sense of relief swept through her. She was safely back in Australia. She didn't have to tell him she was a nurse. She didn't have to talk about any of it.

There were no more emaciated black-skinned bodies. No more hopeless, staring eyes. No more feeling helpless with such few proper facilities to meet horrendous need. No more feeling guilty for being white, for being so well-fed and clothed. No more trying to force herself to keep working to stem the relentless tide of disease and death. No more. . .

Her lips tightened momentarily as she forced the memories away. Soon, very soon, she would really be home. And perhaps then she would be able to sleep. . .deeply. . .dreamlessly. . .

* * *

It was a sudden screech of brakes and Scott's startled exclamation that jolted her awake. She felt her body flung forward against the seatbelt, and then all movement stopped. For a moment she was disorientated. Then, through dazed eyes, she realised the car in front of them had run into the rear of a small truck.

'I'd better see if they need any help.' Scott's voice was grim as he reached into the back seat for a small bag before opening his door. 'No sense in both of us getting wet. You stay here until I see if anyone's hurt badly.'

By the look of the crumpled front and driver's side of the small sedan car, that was a definite possibility.

Jodi shuddered. She knew she should be out there too. She was a nurse, for goodness, sake! But she still sat frozen in her seat, unable to move, watching Scott as he reached the accident. She saw him try to wrench open the driver's crumpled door without success, and then he disappeared around the other side of the car.

A couple of other vehicles had stopped and people were converging on the scene. Jodi relaxed slightly. There were plenty of people to help now. But you have medical experience, her conscience nagged her, especially with trauma injuries.

And then Scott appeared and beckoned to her urgently.

She didn't move. Couldn't move.

He said something to a man beside him and the man turned and started running towards her. By the time he reached the car she had managed to open her door and forced herself out on her trembling legs.

'Doc says he's got a mobile phone,' the man panted, 'and could you go and help him. Got a kid in there. I'll ring for help.'

There was no longer any choice. Jodi took a deep breath and started forward on shaking legs. As she drew closer she heard the screams of a terrified child. She paused momentarily, and then tried desperately to put into operation that inner survival mechanism that had been all that had held her together the past couple of weeks. Scott backed out of the rear of the car and turned towards her as she reached them.

'Here, you take her back to my car,' he rapped out even as he thrust a tiny child at her. 'Scared stiff, but only a few minor cuts as far as I can tell. There's a first-aid kit in the glove box you can use to clean her up.' He glanced up at her as she reached out for the child, and then paused, an arrested look on his face. 'Sure you can cope?'

'Yes, I'll cope,' Jodi said expressionlessly.

He hesitated again, still searching her face, but Jodi clasped the rigid, terrified little body tightly and began stumbling back the way she had come. She deliberately tried to blank out of her mind the crumpled body she had briefly glimpsed sprawled across the front of the crushed dashboard. Despite all her efforts, she knew that it had been covered in glass from the smashed windscreen. And the blood. . .

Jodi shuddered, and desperately blocked off that thought. She put the child down on the seat, and as she reached towards the glove box she saw the blood on her own clothes.

'Oh, no!' she moaned. 'Oh, no! Not again!'

Then her hands were frantically searching, and she almost sobbed with relief as she saw that there was only some bruising where the safety straps had held the little body firmly and the one gash on a plump little leg. She felt as though she was operating on some automatic level as she quickly found the well-stocked first-aid kit, and tried to swab away the trickles of blood from a scratch on the little girl's face and the more serious cut.

'There, there, little one,' Jodi heard herself crooning automatically, managing with considerable difficulty to hold the squirming body still enough to apply a rough gauze dressing to the bleeding gash. 'Just let me cover this up and it'll stop bleeding. Although it might need a little suture later,' she babbled on, 'but you'll be OK. . .hush now. . .'

The toddler's screams gradually subsided after Jodi had cleaned her up as best she could and rocked the soft little body gently against her breast. There was only an occasional quivering sob by the time the sirens heralded the arrival of the ambulance and police.

Jodi saw Scott's tall figure run to the ambulance as it stopped. She closed her eyes tightly, but still the scenario was played out in her mind. No doubt he had been able to arrest any external haemorrhage. But even if there were no serious internal injuries, especially from hitting the steering-wheel or the windscreen, the driver would be shocked as well as in pain. They would need to have to replace the loss of body fluid as soon as possible, ideally with a blood transfusion. But the ambulance would carry some IV fluids.

At least here in this plentiful country there were such basic supplies. Not like that other little hospital. And there had been so much blood. . .so little anyone could do. . .

The little girl in her arms moved jerkily and whimpered. Jodi forced her mind back to her charge, but her hands were shaking as she realised she had tightened her grip on the small body and carefully changed the child's position to a more comfortable place back on her lap. Shock. The child needed more warmth. She glanced around the car helplessly, and then managed to tuck the infant into her own cardigan.

Jodi blanked her mind off again and numbly watched as at last a stretcher was lifted into the gaping end of the ambulance. Scott was there again. This time he glanced towards her, spoke briefly to a man in uniform and then started striding swiftly back to his car.

He was carrying his suit coat as he approached, and he looked somehow even taller in his unbuttoned waistcoat with the long sleeves of his shirt rolled up. And very muscular with those broad shoulders. And very strong, very much in control as he slid into the driver's seat.

'Good girl.' For a moment, Jodi thought he was speaking to the child, and then realised the gleam in his eyes was directed at herself. 'I'm glad you aren't the type of female to faint at the sight of a bit of blood.'

Jodi stared at him blankly. A *bit* of blood. Then her mouth opened, but before she could speak the child gave a whimpering cry as he bent closer to check her. He hastily withdrew as the little tot suddenly clung more fiercely to Jodi and started screaming again.

He hesitated as Jodi tried to soothe her, and then said crisply, 'I was going to put her in the ambulance with her mother, but I think we'd better follow them to the hospital and let you hold her. The paramedic has enough to do. Just a moment.'

He disappeared and she heard the boot of the car open. He reappeared, rubbing at his wet hair with a towel. He tossed a large man's cardigan to her.

'Tuck that around her. Small children are fortunately pretty resilient, but she still must be suffering some shock.'

'She. . .the mother's badly hurt?'

Jodi's voice was hoarse and shaking badly as she wrapped up the little body. She didn't really want to know the answer to her question, but knew she had to ask.

He glanced sharply back at her as he quickly put the car into motion, slipping in behind the ambulance with its lights flashing and siren starting up. 'Are you going to be OK? You're even paler than you were before. . .if that's possible!'

Jodi fought for control, and nodded.

'As far as I can tell, this little tot's mum should be all right,' Scott said abruptly. 'If she'd had her seatbelt done up properly, she wouldn't have hit the windscreen and steering-wheel the way she did,' he added grimly. 'She was fortunate we were in a restricted speed zone and she wasn't moving any faster. As it is she has a fractured leg, some severe bruising where she was crushed against the steering-wheel, and nasty cuts on her face and forearm. But we'd better get her daughter to the hospital too. As soon as she regains consciousness her mum'll be a lot happier with her there. Thank goodness she had this mite in a child's car seat with a good safety harness!'

CHAPTER TWO

THE kookaburra's chortling reached its crescendo. He paused briefly and then started up again.

Jodi didn't stir. Perhaps this time the dream would linger a little longer. Perhaps this time the sounds of home in her dreams wouldn't be replaced too soon by people wailing and crying. . .

A phone distantly shrilled its urgent summons.

Jodi's eyes flew open. The ringing was replaced by the faint murmur of a voice, and then silence. Memory began to penetrate the heaviness of deep sleep.

It had been dusk by the time they had reached the base hospital in Toowoomba, the nearest large hospital to the scene of the accident. Jodi had insisted on staying in the car, even though the little girl had screamed and clung to her as Scott had tried to take her.

Jodi had known he was exasperated with her for not carrying the child into the casualty department, but she had doubted if she could have done so without dropping her anyway. Fatigue had been again washing over her in waves, and despite the chilly air as dark descended she had dozed off again, only stirring briefly as the car had begun moving away from the hospital.

Now, as she sat up stiffly and looked around, she vaguely remembered being lifted from a car by strong arms. A deep voice had murmured soothingly, and she had relaxed again against a firm body that had smelt attractively clean. For the first time in many years she had felt cared for and secure, and had snuggled closer to the warmth and comfort.

There was a faint knock on the door, and then it opened and a tall figure was outlined in the doorway.

'Good, you're awake at last,' a familiar deep voice said. 'I was starting to get worried. Don't move. I'll be back in a sec.' The doorway became empty again.

Jodi sank back obediently on to the pillow automatically, and then jerked upright again. In one movement she threw back the bedclothes and stood up in a panic. A wave of dizziness forced her to plonk down again on the side of the bed.

The accident. The blood. She shuddered, remembering her frantic search of that small body.

She looked down at herself, suddenly realising she was in a clean, old-fashioned flannelette nightie. Jodi felt the trembling in her hands starting up again, and irritably slipped them under her thighs. She looked around her, trying not to think of that other time she had been covered in blood.

It was a very attractive, large bedroom. Sunlight was filtering through the venetian blinds on a large window that almost filled one wall. Frilled curtains were tied back each side beneath a matching swathed pelmet. As she glanced around and then studied the contents on the nearby naturally stained pine dressing-table, she realised it was a very feminine room, although a little too frilly for her taste.

There was a sound out in the corridor, and Jodi watched with dazed eyes as the stranger she had met at the airport entered carrying a steaming cup and a plate. Not really a stranger any more. An unexpected quiver shot through her.

He must be the most handsome 'tall, dark and

handsome' I've ever met, she thought, and then sat up straighter, her shoulders tensing.

'Hope you drink coffee?' Scott said cheerfully as he handed the cup to her and then put the plate next to her on the side-table.

She stared silently at his offering of milky strong coffee and marmalade-covered toast, and then up into dark, intense eyes that were examining her thoroughly.

'How——?' Her voice came out in a husky croak, and she paused and tried to clear her throat, taking the cup and holding it firmly in both hands.

'Our friends in that accident are doing well. Especially your little charge. I rang up first thing,' he said hastily, and then grinned at her. 'You were right when you said you were suffering from jet-lag. You went out like a light.'

Jodi stared at him for a moment, and then quickly averted her eyes, ashamed that it had not been the question she had been going to ask.

His whole face lit up when he smiled, and a quiver of regret flashed through her. Why did she have to meet this attractive man when she was so down, so unattractive, her usually immaculate appearance in total disarray? And, besides her outward appearance, she was not exactly proud of her actions yesterday. She should have told him she was a nurse, and gone and helped him.

'But you're still too pale.'

Jodi glanced back at him. He was frowning thoughtfully at her. 'I'll leave you to have your cuppa in peace. If you feel like it, there's a shower next door. Just use whatever you like, including in the kitchen.' He looked at his watch. 'Afraid I've been called out to a patient, but I shouldn't be long—with a bit of luck!'

'But. . .but where am I?' she managed to call out as he reached the door.

'At Wingeen,' he tossed over his shoulder from the open doorway, 'not too far from Toowoomba. I'll tell you more later.' Then he disappeared even as her mouth flew open again.

She stared after him, heard the distant slam of a door, and then silence. Even the kookaburra was quiet.

'And how. . .who. . .put me to bed?' She muttered the question she'd been starting beforehand, and then felt heat flood her body at the thought of those lean, tanned hands touching her.

'He's a doctor, for goodness' sake,' she said loudly, angrily this time.

She looked down at the cup in her trembling hands, and the strong, delicious aroma was too tempting. Sipping cautiously, she pulled a face. It was much stronger than she liked but sugar had been added to temper the bitterness. After a few more mouthfuls, she stood up and placed it and the plate on the crystal tray on the dressing-table. Munching on a piece of toast, she went over to the window and opened the blinds.

Strong sun streamed into the room as she gasped and stared with delight at the colourful garden spread before her. A mass of gold, white and purple flowers, which she quickly identified as chrysanthemums, were in a bed not far from her against a backdrop of a huge old Chinese amber tree in its fading autumn glory. Beyond the garden and a couple of tall, bluish-green gum trees stretched a dark chocolate ploughed paddock. Beyond that was a patchwork of green and brown paddocks. There was no other house close by and a rather flat-topped small mountain provided a backdrop. This was the country! And furthermore, by the shadows cast across the lawn, it must be close to midday.

Jodi glanced at her watch and gasped again. She had slept for almost twenty hours! Quickly she swallowed the remainder of her drink and toast and made for the bathroom.

By the time Scott Campbell returned, Jodi had showered and dressed in her last clean pair of jeans from her case left thoughtfully in the bedroom. Then she had raided the refrigerator in the cheerful, if untidy kitchen, and was blissfully eating a Vegemite and cheese sandwich with a cup of black, weak tea just as she liked it when she heard the car pull up outside. She didn't move, but as she heard the front door open and footsteps pass the kitchen she called out a little apprehensively, 'I'm in here!'

'Glad you made yourself at home.' Scott smiled as he saw the food in front of her. Then he gave a bark of laughter. 'And that proves you've been out of Australia for a while!'

She glanced down self-consciously. 'I saw and smelt the Vegemite, and just couldn't resist it,' she admitted a little sheepishly.

'Can't stand that black stuff myself, far too salty.' He pulled out a chair opposite her and relaxed with a sigh. 'I've only been away a week and it seems the whole district needs a doctor since very early this morning. Amazing how they always seem to know as soon as I'm home. And now, Jodi, you'd better tell me where you were headed and if anyone will be worried sick about you not arriving.'

'Well, I've tried ringing my brother again with no answer,' Jodi said with a frown. 'I can't understand it.'

Scott suddenly took a deep breath. 'So Jimmy is your brother.'

There was a rather strange look on his face when Jodi glanced up at him. She felt warmth touch her as she remembered he had thought she was being met by her boyfriend.

She opened her mouth again, but Scott continued in an even-toned voice, 'Whereabouts does he live? If it's not too far, and patients permitting, perhaps I can take you there.'

'Oh, I'm sure he or Ann will come and get me if I can contact him. Do you mind if I try them again?'

A few minutes later, Jodi rejoined Scott with a worried frown. 'There's still no one answering. Perhaps they've been away and didn't get my cable.' She hesitated, and added, 'Do. . .do you know where Kingsluck is?'

Scott's eyebrows shot up. 'The Kingsluck estate? That's a rural small acreage subdivision. It's just north-west of us.' Scott's expression suddenly changed again. 'You said your name's Banner, didn't you? Is your brother David Banner by any chance?'

The sudden sharpness in his voice chilled her. She nodded. 'Yes, David James. I've always called him Jimmy, but——' She broke off as Scott suddenly leaned forward and propped his chin on his hands, studying her intently.

As he stared at her, she noted the expression in his dark brown eyes harden. 'And you, perhaps, are the little sister he called Jo!'

There was so much scorn in his voice that she stared back at him in bewilderment.

'His little *nursing* sister,' the deep voice drawled slowly.

'Oh!' Jodi felt the crimson tide flood her face and she stared blindly down at the empty plate in front of her, and when he didn't speak she glanced up at him. 'I. . .I should have told you at the accident,' she said in flat tones. Then she straightened her shoulders defiantly. 'I told you I was tired.'

'Too tired to help in an emergency?'

'Yes!' she heard herself snap back. 'And tired of people who are sick and dying, and doctors who expect. . .expect. . .'

Her fist went up to her mouth to stem the flow of words. She stared angrily at him.

His face softened a little. He ran his hand suddenly through his dark hair. 'I guess I can identify with that feeling only too well.' His face hardened. 'But still, it was an emergency situation,' he added abruptly as he stood up.

'I. . .I just couldn't. . .couldn't——' Jodi broke off again and squeezed her eyes tightly shut for a moment, but she still felt the wretched tears start trickling down her face. She brushed them angrily away. 'I'm sorry about yesterday, but, believe me, I would have been more hindrance than help.' She took a deep breath and glared at him. 'But if you know my brother, perhaps you know where he might be?'

'No, I don't,' Scott said shortly. 'They brought their little daughter to me with an asthma attack, and I discovered he was an accountant. We've met a few times since, and he's agreed to do some bookwork for me. I've been away myself, but I'm sure someone else in this small community will know. Wait here and I'll try and find out.'

He returned while she was still tidying the kitchen. 'They're away on holidays,' he said abruptly in answer to her anxious look. 'I found his business card and rang where he works in Toowoomba. They said he was taking his family up to Cairns.'

That only too familiar, terrible feeling of rejection and helplessness filled Jodi's eyes with more tears. She felt her body begin to shake, and saw alarm flash into Scott's face.

Then he was across the room saying swiftly, 'It's all right, Jo. You'll be fine,' and suddenly he pulled her into his arms as he said rapidly, 'I'll look after you. They've already been gone a week. They said he shouldn't be away more than another couple of weeks at the most.'

She relaxed against him, and vaguely she was reminded of the strength and comfort she had experienced the night before in his arms. He held her for a moment, and then she felt his hands move up under her hair to cradle the back of her head. She tensed, and then wrenched herself away.

His hands dropped to his sides and they stared at each other. Electricity leapt between them. Then Scott's lips tightened and he turned away towards the window.

'What do you want to do, then? Are you going to wait around here for them?' he tossed over his shoulder in even tones.

'I. . .I don't know,' stammered Jodi, still feeling bewildered by the sudden tension between them. 'No. I can't stay here, though,' she added quickly.

'Why not?'

His abrupt words brought her head up. 'Because the lady whose bed I occupied last night might not like an unexpected guest.'

He stared silently out of the window for a moment

longer, and then turned slowly to face her. His eyes were narrowed as he considered her for a moment. 'But then, you don't know my aunt Edith.'

'Your aunt lives here with you?'

'No, she doesn't live here with me. She lives here. It's her house. I'm only staying while she's away.'

'But aren't you the local doctor?' She frowned, trying to remember if he had said anything else in the car.

'I'm just doing a locum for a friend of my aunt.'

His eyes twinkled unexpectedly. Something stirred deep inside her, and she stared at him again, fascinated by the way his smile lit his dark face.

I could become addicted to watching the slow spreading of a smile on his face, she thought unexpectedly. It starts in his eyes long before his lips move. And then that dimple makes a brief appearance sometimes. Jodi pulled herself together as she realised he was speaking again.

'In fact, he's no longer just her friend. She married him a couple of months ago and they took off on a world trip for a honeymoon. So that makes him my uncle. It left rather a gap in the medical services to this community. Not only was he the only local doctor, she was the district nurse,' he added, and then paused before murmuring, 'Seen anything you like?'

With a start, Jodi realised her eyes had followed the line of his strong jaw and the movement of his throat as he'd talked, and then dropped to where his open-necked shirt showed a dark tan. . .and lower. . .to slim hips. . .

Her eyes flew back to his face. His eyes were twinkling devilishly although his mouth was straight. And then his last soft words penetrated, and she went hot all over.

'Is. . .are the surgery rooms near by?' she blurted out hurriedly.

He didn't answer her for several long moments as he let his own gaze slide over the curves even her well-washed green T-shirt couldn't disguise, and down over the jeans that hung loosely on her once shapely form. His eyes had lost all trace of amusement, but were very thoughtful, when they returned to examine her face and the dark auburn hair now lacklustre and streaked by a relentless sun. One dark eyebrow rose as he dwelt on the hollows on her cheeks and the dark rings under her eyes before locking with her hazel eyes again.

It had been a long time since a man had so blatantly surveyed her, but she had definitely been surveying him first, and so she lifted her head higher as she straightened. She opened her mouth but he spoke first.

'When the public-minded citizens of this area decided a few years ago they wanted their own doctor instead of travelling to Oakey or Toowoomba, my aunt offered them the use of rooms here,' he said slowly. 'It's an old farmhouse meant for a large family, and with a wide veranda on three sides. They enclosed some of that to make more waiting and storage space.'

He paused, still considering Jodi thoughtfully. 'Her first husband farmed the land around here before he died. She was a registered nursing sister and helped the doctor out at times, and then when my uncle died the community extended their medical services to include a district nurse and employed her. That was some years ago, and now the locals are finding it very hard to adjust without her.' He hesitated, and then moved closer. 'She resigned when they were married. We haven't been successful in replacing her yet.'

Jodi froze, suddenly knowing what his next words would be.

'Have you got a job to return to or would you like to work with me for a few weeks?'

CHAPTER THREE

JODI was already shaking her head before he had finished speaking. 'No, I don't want to be a nurse any more,' she said coldly, and as firmly as she could.

His eyes narrowed. 'Had a bad time at your last job?'

She closed her eyes briefly, and then nodded jerkily before looking back at him.

'So, what do you want to do now?' he asked her quietly after a moment. 'I really do think you should stay here until you're more recovered from. . .' He paused and then said firmly, 'From your holiday. Just where have you been, Jodi? I noticed a Qantas sticker on your case, and one I think must be African.'

'Yes,' she said shortly, 'Africa.' She took a deep breath and continued in a very controlled voice. 'And it wasn't a holiday. I've been working with a church missionary organisation in a pretty remote area. One of the more recent refugee camps.'

She told him the name of it. His eyebrows shot up, and his eyes widened. Obviously he had heard news reports from there, but she very much doubted if the last few days had filtered through yet.

'But I'd prefer not to talk about it just now,' she added abruptly.

'Or you can't talk about it?'

Jodi was silent, staring at him, noticing the gentle understanding that entered his face. Swallowing the sudden lump in her throat, she said huskily, 'I've got other things to talk about now.'

She put a little more distance between them, and added in a stronger voice, 'My brother sent me a key to his house a few years ago when they first moved here. It. . .it was a fun thing, he said,' she continued hurriedly, remembering her amusement at his gesture, but suddenly wondering if he had known even then that one day she would give up trying to live at peace with their father. 'But I'm sure they wouldn't mind if I used it and stayed there until they returned.'

There was no movement behind her, and at last she ventured to glance at him.

The dark frown was back on his face. 'I'm not sure that's a wise thing to do, if, as you told me, you've been sick, and you've recently had a bad time. Their house in that area is probably on a small acreage, and there wouldn't be any neighbours really close.'

Jodi swung around. 'I. . .I haven't really been sick, just exhausted. I can manage very well by myself,' she said steadily. 'So, if you wouldn't mind——'

She stopped abruptly as they heard the blare of a car horn. Scott's head lifted, and then he was hurrying from the room. She hesitated briefly, and then followed, reaching the front veranda as he went bounding down the steps towards a battered station wagon pulling to a hasty stop.

A frantic-faced, elderly man sprang from the car. 'My wife's burnt herself. . .and busted her leg real bad,' he called out as he rounded the car to where Scott was already opening the back passenger door.

Jodi took a very deep, very shaky breath, and then found herself moving slowly down the steps.

A small, grey-faced woman was propped up against the door in the back with both legs up on the car seat. They were covered by a wet sheet, and Jodi's breath caught as Scott carefully folded it back. It only took one glance to see the large reddened areas and blisters on both legs from the knees to the ankles. One ankle was also very swollen. She was watching them from dazed, pain-filled eyes.

'Vera Wood, what have you been doing to yourself now?' Scott's calm voice was filled with gentle concern. 'Excitement of another new grandchild gone to your head?' he teased, but his hands were quickly examining the swollen ankle.

'I. . .I was taking her straight to the hospital. Didn't know you was home,' the man said shakily. 'Then. . . then we saw your car here and. . .and she said stop here first. . .'

'And just as well,' Scott said calmly. 'I can make her a bit more comfortable for the rest of the trip. Jodi, if you follow the front veranda around to our left, you'll come to the surgery. First door. My black bag's on the desk at the reception desk.'

His voice had only sharpened a little, but Jodi found herself responding to the urgent undertones instinctively by flying back up the steps. The bag was where he said in the small waiting-room, and her prompt return earned her a brief smile, even as he said comfortingly to Mrs Wood, 'You're fortunate I've just returned from another emergency, Vera, and my bag of tricks has just what you need first.'

He very rapidly drew up an ampoule of morphia and shot it into her arm.

'Th-thanks, Scott,' the woman gasped.

'Shush, now,' he said cheerfully. 'Just try and relax. You'll be feeling much better very soon. We need to get you to hospital to treat these burns, and X-ray that ankle, but I don't think we'll try and move you.

Bill's done an excellent job packing you into this car, so we'll take you the rest of the way as you are. But I think we'll put in a drip to be on the safe side. Jodi Banner here is a nurse and she'll take a few observations while I make a phone call and get some equipment.'

Jodi tensed angrily. Once again he was the arrogant man she had first met at the airport.

He jerked his head significantly at Jodi and then climbed out of the car. She hesitated briefly, and then apprehensively followed him from her place hanging over the front seat as he said briskly to the woman's husband, 'Best to get into the front seat and stay with her for a couple of minutes, Bill. We won't be long.'

As the man took her place in the car, Scott added softly and rapidly to Jodi, 'My sphygmo's in my bag. Sorry to load this on to you, but if I'm going to put in a drip I'll need you to sit back there with her to hold it. Bill's in no state to drive. We could wait for an ambulance but it has to come from Toowoomba. She's pretty shocked and the sooner we get her to the base the better. OK?'

Jodi knew she had no choice, and reluctantly gave a little nod. The sudden sweetness of his smile made her catch her breath and she turned hastily back to climb into the rear of the wagon. Heat swept through her as she heard a whispered 'Atta girl!' behind her.

When Scott climbed back into the car, she silently handed him the notepad she had found in his bag. He glanced briefly at the dangerously lowered blood-pressure reading and rapid pulse, and nodded briefly.

'As I thought. We'll get some saline into her. Casualty is expecting us. I grabbed this blanket for her too.'

Jodi noticed the woman was shivering a little from the shock as she tucked the blanket around her upper body, leaving one arm free.

Babies, old people, so susceptible to shock. A tremor passed through her. Scott had been lifting the tray he was carrying towards her, and paused.

'Are you all right?'

She nodded abruptly and almost snatched the tray. Without looking at him, she positioned it on the hard surface on the floor beside her, and leaned over the back seat as he began to explain to Vera what he was going to do.

'Bill,' he said gently to the man anxiously peering at them from the front seat, 'why don't you go back into the house and get some cushions out of the lounge-room? Jodi will have to stay in the back, and it might help her be a bit more comfortable on the trip to town.'

Jodi handed a cannula to Scott while she reluctantly stretched over the seat to put the tourniquet on Vera's arm. Her trembling hands betrayed her again, but he merely flashed her another penetrating glance before bending to his task of finding a vein.

Finding a vein in a plump arm was never easy, especially when the vein was a little flat from shock. Jodi had worked with many members of the medical fraternity over the years and couldn't help admiring the speed and efficiency with which he inserted the cannula, especially in such cramped conditions.

By the time the cannula had been strapped into place, Jodi had inserted the IV line into the saline sachet, filled the line with fluid and clamped it off ready for him to attach. She held it as high as she could, and in no time at all the fluid was dripping steadily.

'Now, we can't elevate this the way we should, so you and Bill will have to take turns in holding it as high and still as you can,' Scott said crisply. He glanced over his shoulder as Bill joined them, and added, 'I hope you don't mind if I drive the rest of the way, Bill?'

The relief on the old worn face as Bill nodded made Jodi bite back her instinctive protest that the two men could manage. Obviously the man needed someone else to drive. He was almost as pale as his wife.

Why don't I feel more sympathy for them both? Jodi thought helplessly as she felt the familiar dull pain in her head which heralded the commencement of one of her far too frequent headaches. Somewhere along the way these last few days it was as though her emotions had somehow been blunted when it came to a patient's suffering.

'Thank goodness you're back, Doc,' Bill said fervently as Scott climbed out of his cramped place in the car. 'I've told her and told her not to carry boiling water down those rickety back steps.'

Scott smiled at the elderly couple as he said cheerfully, 'So am I glad to be back, believe me! Now, Bill, you hang on to this bag of saline while Jodi gets as comfortable as she can in the back and we'll be on our way.'

It was a fairly slow trip to start with. The narrow strip of bitumen that wound around the farms had been corroded in places, and it was a relief when they at last came out on to the main western highway to Toowoomba. Jodi held the saline sachet for most of the trip, and by the time they reached the hospital was feeling stiff and aching from her cramped position, despite the cushions on the hard floor of the back of the station wagon.

It was difficult keeping the flow-rate regulated, and Jodi was very relieved when her responsibilities ended. The transfer to a trolley was accomplished with a few low moans of pain from the unfortunate woman.

Bill was standing near Jodi as she stretched her cramped muscles. Together they watched the hospital wardsman start the trolley towards the nearby casualty entrance, the saline now secure on the trolley's stand. Scott was close on their heels, all his attention on his patient.

'My poor, poor old girl,' Jodi heard Bill mutter in a choked voice.

She turned towards him and saw him sway for a moment. Before she could move, he gave a soft moan, and then a choking sound as he collapsed in a crumpled heap.

'Scott!' she called urgently.

Then she was on her knees beside the old man. For a brief moment as he had gone down she'd thought he had only fainted. But her years of experience told her, as she rolled him on to his back and saw his congested face, it was far more than that.

Automatically her fingers sought for the pulse in his carotid artery. As her fingers left his neck and flew to rip open his shirt, Scott was beside them.

'No pulse,' she snapped.

Her mind clicked into automatic gear. Position the patient on his back. Head extended. Actually witnessed arrest. Not a minute since he went down. She gave Bill's chest the pre-cordial thump with her fist.

The wardsman had paused briefly, looking back over his shoulder.

'Cardiac arrest!' roared Scott, even as he was intent on extending Bill's head and holding his jaw.

The wardsman deserted the trolley and disappeared inside the open doors fast.

It was as though they had worked together many times before. They both had done CPR before, but never together as now, always with other participants. Scott kept the head extended and held the jaw firmly so the airway remained clear. At the same time Jodi placed both her hands in the correct position on the sternum, elbows straight.

She started counting each compression softly out loud, her brain automatically registering Scott delivering the first two quick breaths into the lungs. Then the rhythm took over. Five down. One breath. Don't pause as ventilation given. Five. One. Am I pressing down hard enough? Scott's hands keeping the airway clear. Scott checking the carotid again.

Then the wardsman returned with a nurse.

'Got the air viva,' he gasped breathlessly, adding, 'have to get back to the lady on the trolley,' and disappeared again fast.

'Arrest team alerted,' his companion said curtly.

Jodi vaguely registered that the nurse was attaching a mask to the bag. Scott snatched it from her. Then it was in place to squeeze for the next ventilation.

No break in the compressions. Press. Another five. Ventilation. Getting tired far too quickly.

Scott murmured to the nurse who had her fingers now on the femoral artery. The nurse took Scott's place.

'Right. My turn.'

Scott's large hands quickly replaced Jodi's, with hardly a break in the rhythm. She crouched on the ground opposite him silently, breathless, but ready to relieve again if needed.

The rhythm continued for seemingly endless moments. Suddenly the cardiac arrest team were there. But there was a murmur from the nurse now squeezing the bag and checking the carotid. Scott paused. Jodi stumbled a few paces to collapse against the car and watch as a white-coated figure pressed a stethoscope to the heart. Other hands were slipping on the leads to the Life-Pak's monitor.

'Got him,' a voice said cheerfully, and there was a brief, instant relief of tension.

'And easily within three minutes,' Scott murmured with satisfaction as he checked his watch, and Jodi realised with a swiftly indrawn breath that she had completely forgotten to note the time of the arrest. So important to assess any possible brain damage.

A brief pause as the vital signs were checked. Then a trolley was there, and, very quickly, willing hands carefully lifted the still unconscious man on to it, and then the entrance was empty.

Jodi slumped against the car, one fist pressed to her mouth, trying to stop its quivering. Slow tears started to trickle from her closed eyes down on to her cheeks. Angrily she brushed them away. 'I didn't need that. I really didn't need that.'

She only realised she had said the words aloud when Scott's voice said crisply, 'And neither did Bill.'

She jerked her head away, but a large hand grasped her jaw and gently, but firmly, turned her head back towards him. He studied her ravaged face for a moment. Then he gave a big sigh, and gathered her up and hugged her.

'You were great, just great,' he murmured in her hair.

Jodi's tension began to flow from her, and she buried

her head closer into his broad shoulder. She'd read somewhere once that every person needed a certain number of hugs a day. At the time she had been scornful, quickly suppressing the twinge of self-pity because there had been no one to hug her on a regular basis. She could really get used to having this man around.

Just for hugs?

Jodi pulled herself free, and shakily accepted the handkerchief pressed into her hand.

'I don't believe this! I've hardly been off the plane five minutes, and been involved in three emergencies!' She tried to sound indignant, but just sounded as shaky as she felt.

Scott's lips twitched slightly. 'And you've done very well. . .' His pause was covered up smoothly by his adding rapidly, 'Today!'

'You think I've done well!' she exclaimed. 'I'm a cot case. And I worked in IC for five years!'

'Five years! They say not many survive three in intensive care work without burning out! But no wonder you were so spot-on starting CPR. Pre-cordial thumps aren't given very often these days. Not enough actually witness the arrest.'

'I've only ever been on the spot once before too. And I didn't burn out in IC, as you put it,' she snapped defensively, wondering, not for the first time these past few weeks, if that was strictly true!

'I'm glad to hear it,' Scott said blandly. 'Come on, we both need a cup of coffee.'

'I hate coffee!'

'Tea, then.'

Jodi shook her head abruptly.

'Nevertheless, you're having some,' Scott said firmly.

'No,' snapped Jodi. 'I'll wait for you out here.'

'Jodi, you haven't recovered from your trip, and you've had a shock. Now, you either walk inside, or I'll carry you.'

Jodi's mouth dropped. The words had been said in a conversational manner, but the stubborn look in his eyes and the tilt of his firm jaw told her he would have no hesitation in picking her up.

'You're impossible,' she grumbled.

'Yes, I know,' he said cheerfully, and held out his hand.

Almost before she knew it, she found her own tucked into his, and then they were walking towards the hospital.

He must have felt her tension increase as they walked past the waiting patients, and his hand tightened on hers.

'They were taking Bill straight up to Intensive Care,' Scott said softly. 'I've got to park the car and then write up a few things for the staff here about Vera. We'll check on them both before we leave. There's a small waiting-room nearby. You can wait for me there.'

He collected a drink for her on the way, but when they reached the waiting-room there was not a seat to spare.

'Look, Scott,' Jodi said hurriedly as they turned away, 'I really would prefer to wait in the car.'

Scott ran a hand through his hair. He stopped, and studied her carefully. 'Are you sure you're OK now?'

'Of course I am!' she said aggressively.

He sighed in defeat. 'You drive?'

When she had nodded abruptly he said autocratically, 'The car's still in the ambulance bay. You can park it for me, and then wait on one of the seats just outside the arrival area.'

Not even so much as a 'please', seethed Jodi silently.

'No,' she said sharply with her chin elevated, 'I'll park the car and wait for you there.'

Jodi could feel the tension back in her shoulders and her headache was beginning to throb. That dreadful shaky feeling was also invading her limbs again as she started to move away.

'You'll need these.'

She turned back at his exasperated snap, and snatched at the keys he was holding out. Unexpectedly, he grabbed her extended hand, and before she knew it pulled her close, bent over and gave her a brief but mind-spinning kiss on the lips.

There were a few cat-calls and wolf-whistles from the suddenly less bored people in the waiting area.

He grinned devastatingly at her. She started blushing furiously. He touched one finger to her lips, 'Nice,' he murmured, and then she was staring after his broad back as it moved swiftly away.

Jodi avoided meeting any of the eyes watching them either gleefully, or, she had no doubt, disapprovingly, and stormed towards the entrance. The hide of him! But her lips tingled still, and she rubbed at them with her hand.

One part of her wanted to see the layout of this large public hospital, the other wanted nothing to do with it at all. Will this abhorrence of anything and everything to do with nursing and medicine go away or is it only temporary? Jodi wondered despairingly.

Had her father been right all those years ago when he had snarled out that nursing would never be challenging enough for her? At the time she had dismissed his contempt as only part of his bitter disappointment that she, like David, had refused to follow in his footsteps and become a doctor.

No, she decided abruptly after she had managed to find an empty car space to park the car, and began tidying up the back seat so that she could curl up there herself. Nursing, if anything, had been too much of a challenge for her. Her lips curled in self-derision as she relaxed at last with a sigh of relief and closed her eyes.

Her father hadn't bothered to write to her once while she had been in Africa. It had been no more than she had expected after that last blazing row when she had refused point-blank to cancel her trip. Without her knowledge, he had still been engineering an opening for her to re-apply to do medicine. He had several influential friends, but doing that behind her back had shown her his continuing contempt for her nursing career. And it had all added to her sense of worthlessness in his eyes.

She didn't want to dwell on all that had happened the last year, and deliberately forced her thoughts back to her immediate problem. There was no way she wanted to go crawling back home to open herself up again to her father's scorn and anger. And there was no way she could stay in the same house with a doctor. Even one as attractive as Scott, the unbidden thought came.

Her eyes flew open, and she stared blindly across the car park. He had handled Vera and Bill very well, showing the traits she had always looked for in a doctor. He had been firm, competent, decisive, but also understanding and compassionate. Deliberately she shut off the admission that there was anything about that bossy man that drew her, and tried to remember all that her brother had said about his home.

Jimmy had definitely mentioned having some poultry, for he had told her about collecting the eggs once and nearly stepping on a snake also on the same quest. Then, hadn't there been some reference to a cow Ann had insisted on buying? Buttercup. Yes, that was its name because she could remember grinning about their playing at being farmers.

She was wondering briefly who was looking after the animals for her brother when Scott returned. He opened the driver's door and his lips quirked as he surveyed the way she had made herself comfortable.

'I thought you'd be ages,' she said defensively as she swung her legs down and sat up.

'Nope,' he said cheerfully. 'I just wrote an admission letter for the resident medical officer so they know what time she had the morphia and what time we started the saline. She has to be admitted as a public patient, so is no longer my responsibility. It took me longer to find you in this big car park. Now, seeing it's almost lunchtime, we're going to have a bit of a look around the city and then have a picnic in the gardens.'

She frowned. 'Wouldn't it better to go and find my brother's place?'

'Well, I want to call back here and see how Vera and Bill are before we go back home. If Vera's up to it, I need to ask her what arrangements to make about their animals back home as well as this car.'

'Oh.' Jodi bit her lip. 'Do they have any family?'

'A son on the Gold Coast. He'll be contacted by the staff. Now, come on. Get into the front, and we'll see what you think of Toowoomba as a place to live.'

Jodi glanced sideways at him curiously as he started the car. Why was such an obviously competent doctor doing a locum, and not have his own practice or a permanent job somewhere?

Perhaps this would be an opportunity to find out a bit about this strikingly handsome man, as arrogant as he was. After all, she had enjoyed that hug. But it was the sweetness of that very public kiss that was the hardest to forget!

CHAPTER FOUR

JODI'S headache had eased somewhat, and at first she enjoyed the unexpected drive around the city.

'I didn't realise how hungry I've been to see green lawns and trees. No wonder they call Toowoomba The Garden City!' she exclaimed, after they had been driving through beautiful camphor-laurel-tree-lined streets, and then past a large tree- and garden-filled park which Scott told her was Queen's Park.

'And this is the end of May,' remarked Scott. 'You should have been here for their Carnival of Flowers last September. The whole town seems to get involved. The gardens are really superb then, from those owned by the council to the private ones around homes. Shops, organisations, churches all enter into the spirit of it with decorating their premises, and decorating floats for the procession.'

Jodi had heard a little from one of the infrequent letters from David, and now she understood one of the reasons why they loved the area so much.

'You were here last year?' Jodi asked curiously. 'Isn't this rather a long time to do a locum?'

He gave a slight laugh. 'I was only on holidays then. Visiting Aunt Edith. I didn't have a clue her doctor friend was looking me over to see if he dared leave his beloved patients at the mercy of Edith's nephew, even though I grew up on the black soil plains west of here. I've only been in Sydney since my last year in high school. Douglas is a partner in a practice on the outskirts of the city. He prefers to live here and look after the rural side.'

Puzzled, Jodi frowned and turned to look at him. 'But how come you're free to do a locum? Don't you have a permanent job?'

She saw his body tense. His hands tightened their grip on the steering-wheel.

'Thank you for the implied compliment! Yes, I had a job, a very good one, in fact. Surgical registrar. Edith knew I was looking for a change.' The words were clipped and cold, tinged with a trace of bitterness.

Rebuffed, Jodi bit her lip and turned her face away. He obviously didn't want to talk to her about himself. But she couldn't help wondering why he'd been looking for a change.

Then, for some reason, she remembered his words at the airport. He was 'off' all females. Some woman had upset him. Perhaps thrown him over? Somehow Jodi doubted that any woman in her right mind would do that to such a caring, sexy man.

She pulled up her thoughts sharply, and murmured appreciatively as Scott pointed out the turn-off of the highway to Brisbane.

'A very steep road down the range,' he said lightly, and went on to explain how Toowoomba was perched on the top of a range of mountains with a sharp drop on its eastern side, and the foothills of The Great Dividing Range rolling gently towards the fertile western plains of the Darling Downs. They got out of the car at a beautifully landscaped picnic and look-out area called simply Picnic Point.

She tensed for a moment as Scott reached for her hand, but then reluctantly curled her own thin fingers around his large hand, and let him lead her down some steps to stroll along the path that had sweeping panoramas of the Lockyer valley stretching towards the east. It was still a perfect, sunny afternoon with hardly a breeze. Not far away a chicken hawk hovered briefly and then swooped down on its prey, past the treetops and cliffs, and then out of sight.

Death even in such a peaceful place, Jodi thought drearily, and shuddered.

Scott glanced at her sharply, and his clasp on her hand tightened. Suddenly its warmth was strangely comforting as he pointed out glimpses of the Brisbane highway winding its way down the valley. A large semi-trailer appeared briefly and looked like a mere matchbox toy.

'That's the way we came last night,' Scott said slowly. 'There've been many severe accidents on that stretch of road down the range over the years, especially when it was only one lane each way years ago.'

But the fleeting sense of pleasure Jodi had found in the excursion had disappeared. Memories of the previous day intruded, and worry about what she was going to do.

Scott kept up a cheerful commentary as they left Picnic Point and drove north to the large water reservoir on Mount Kynoch, but Jodi felt the familiar grey feeling pressing down on her. The headache increased with a vengeance. She had to force herself to respond appropriately to the sweeping view from that look-out over the city, and the gently undulating farmlands that swept westwards back towards Kingsluck.

She had not realised how quiet she had become until Scott said remorsefully as they returned to the car, 'That wind was chilly, and I've tired you out again.'

She opened her mouth to deny it, but then paused. A feeling of defeat swept through her. 'Yes, I'm afraid I am rather weary still,' she said listlessly.

She was aware that Scott glanced at her thoughtfully as he waited for a gap in the traffic to drive out on to the highway. He was quiet until they pulled into the car park of a take-away food place.

'You wait in the car. I won't be long,' he said with a slight smile.

Briefly, she knew she should feel indignant. He could have at least asked for her preference. But she couldn't be bothered feeling anything. It didn't really matter. She wasn't hungry anyway.

But that was something Scott would have none of after they had parked next to the botanical gardens.

'Come on,' he insisted firmly, 'there's a lovely sheltered spot here. And you haven't had anything since that sandwich.'

And it was lovely. The gardens also still had beautiful autumn colouring and bright flowerbeds. A few roses bloomed stubbornly on their bushes, despite the imminence of winter.

Jodi tried to shake off her sombre mood as Scott spread out their picnic of salad and barbecued chicken on the picnic table between them. But, as had happened so many times these last few weeks, she had no appetite. Nevertheless, she accepted the food he handed her and made an effort to eat.

They were silent for a while in the peaceful surroundings, only disturbed by the cheerful noise of a couple of small children playing nearby. Then a wild throw brought their large ball bouncing perilously close.

Jodi tensed. Scott called cheerfully to them as he moved swiftly to stop it bouncing into a garden bed, and then bowled it back to them. They ran off giggling as Scott collapsed back on the bench.

'They'll never know how fortunate they are.'

The words burst from that deep well within Jodi that she thought she had managed to suppress. She stiffened, and looked down at the piece of chicken in her hand, aware that Scott was very still.

'That sounded very bitter, Jodi.'

The words were quiet, but with an inflexion in them that brought her eyes to his face. He was frowning, his lips a straight line. Her heart gave an unexpected lurch. She moistened her suddenly dry lips, but was unable to speak. .

He suddenly put down the food in his hand. 'I've been told I'm a very good listener if you'd like to talk about any problems you have, Jodi.'

Jodi straightened jerkily and stared at him. Her face lost every bit of colour. They were almost the identical words that the grey-haired mission director had said compassionately to her after she had only been at the refugee camp hospital a few weeks.

Sudden, bitter regret flooded through her. Perhaps if she had shared then what had driven her to resign her position as the nursing unit manager of that intensive care unit in Sydney, she might have been better able to handle the ensuing weeks.

Instead, the stress had built up and up until there had been far too many days when it had taken a supreme effort of will to drag herself out of bed most mornings. Days when she hadn't wanted even to lift a mug of water to the lips of one more sick person. Days when headaches had been her constant companion. And then, these last couple of weeks, she knew she would never have survived if she had not forced herself to switch off her reaction to those she had been forced to care for.

Now she suddenly wondered for the first time if she had actually reached her limit of endurance even before going to Africa. Long before this last traumatic couple of weeks.

'Jodi, sometimes we have to talk to someone to release our tension, or our stress levels can reach dangerous heights.'

There was a lengthy pause while she searched his dark eyes. They were gentle with concern and a depth of understanding for her, Jodi Banner, that she didn't ever remember seeing in anyone's eyes before, not even the mission director.

A hard lump lodged in her throat and when she eventually tried to speak her voice sounded harsh. 'I. . .I know,' she said briefly, 'but. . .but you're a stranger.'

'Sometimes it's easier to talk to strangers than those who think they know all about us.'

Silently and painfully she acknowledged the truth of his words. Her eyes suddenly felt burning and painful. She squeezed them shut. 'You might be right,' she whispered with difficulty, 'but I don't think I can. . . not yet. . .'

There was a pause, and then her eyes flew open as he said very quietly, 'Whenever you're ready, I'll be there.'

His eyes were hidden this time as she searched his face. She could tell little from its expression. A faint frown still creased his forehead, and then eased as the children suddenly ran towards them again. Scott caught their wayward ball, but this time just tossed it silently back, and then picked up his piece of chicken and bit off another mouthful.

'Come on, eat up. It's getting late if we're going to find your brother's place. And we need to see how our patients are first.'

Jodi winced, but was silent. She didn't have any patients, she wanted to snarl at him, but was silent. Having patients meant having to look after them, care about their whole well-being, and she didn't want to have to do that any more.

As they neared the hospital later, Jodi realised how thankful she was that Bill had arrested when they had reached the hospital, and her involvement then had really only been very brief.

Scott unexpectedly echoed her own thought, but with a different motive. 'Just as well Bill hung on until we reached Cas,' he suddenly said as they stopped. 'I knew he had a heart condition. That's why I drove them to the hospital.' He swung his door open. 'I shouldn't be long.'

She was glad he hadn't tried to get her to go with him again. But he was wrong about not being away long. By the time she saw him striding swiftly back, she was so cold she was almost ready to go inside merely to get warm.

'Sorry,' he said briefly. 'Bill's still not too good. He arrested again in IC. They were forced to tell Vera and she took it badly. The staff haven't been able to get hold of their son yet. Vera wants me to ring their next-door neighbour to ask them to look after the farm until he gets here.'

Jodi shivered.

'You stupid girl! You're frozen. Why on earth didn't

you wait inside?' He scowled as he started the car heater.

Jodi found there was just no answer to that, and it was a silent drive back to Wingeen. Scott obviously cared a great deal about his elderly friends. Jodi glanced occasionally at his stern profile, but held her tongue.

'I'm sorry, but I won't have time to take you over to your brother's place now,' he said curtly as he stopped the car. 'I've surgery here this evening, and several things to do first, so I hope you don't mind looking after yourself again.'

Jodi suddenly felt a little confused at the wave of relief she felt at his abrupt words. She had been longing to be by herself for a while. There was so much she needed to sort out in her mind.

But her head was now aching abominably, and she wouldn't have to worry about getting in food tonight and finding her way around a strange house. The fact that she would no longer have Scott near by had nothing to do with it, she assured herself quickly as she followed him slowly into the house.

Jodi went straight to her room and lay down with weary relief. She had been afraid he might ask her to help him with the inevitable stream of patients who would no doubt arrive to see him after his absence. So she stayed in her room until she had heard his tread going to his office before venturing out. She wandered into the lounge and switched on the TV, trying not to think about how many cars and people she heard arriving and departing.

But as it grew late she felt a sense of guilt that was enough at last to make her go and forage in his refrigerator for something to eat for them both. There were a few frozen precooked casseroles in single servings, and when she eventually heard him enter the kitchen two of them had been heated in the microwave and she had set one end of the kitchen table for two.

'Oh, great!' he said appreciatively. 'Was that one full surgery tonight! Nice not to have to get my own tea as well.'

Jodi bit her lip. For a moment she regretted not offering her help, but threw off the feeling as she said abruptly, 'They were in the freezer. I only had to heat them.'

'I know,' he said slowly as he pulled out a chair and sank wearily into it. 'Vera keeps me stocked up well. Or she did. I suppose I'll have to try and replace her tomorrow too.'

At her look of enquiry, he added simply, 'She's been looking after me. House-cleaning, laundry, cooking.'

He must have caught the derisive look in her eyes for he gave a short snort. 'And yes, I know I should be quite capable of doing all those things myself! But there just hasn't been time. I've been doing some of my aunt's run as well as the practice. Quite a few of my patients tonight were some of hers.'

Jodi tensed, waiting for him to try and persuade her again to take the job of district nurse. Instead, after she had served their meal, she was astounded as he very naturally and simply bowed his head and gave thanks for their food, adding a prayer for the Woods.

'By the way,' he said as he started eating without looking at her, 'I just rang the hospital, and they're both doing well now. Both in Intensive Care for at least tonight, but I was assured they were fine.'

Jodi murmured appropriately, but stared down at her plate, suddenly appalled at herself. She quite honestly had not given another thought to the old couple all evening. Can't I care what happens to anyone any more? she asked herself helplessly. Once she would have rung the hospital herself.

'What's wrong, Jo?'

She raised frightened eyes to see Scott observing her with a worried frown. Tears gathered behind her eyes.

'I. . . I've got a headache and I'm not very hungry,' she muttered.

'No,' he said flatly, 'something just upset you. Was it the Woods? Or. . .I hope it wasn't my saying grace.'

She continued to stare at him, and it wasn't until she saw his eyes widen and glance down her face that she realised tears had started to roll down her cheeks.

'Oh, Scott,' she whispered in a shaking voice, 'I don't know what's happening to me any more. It scares me.' Her voice rose. 'I don't seem to care any more. Not about that woman, or the baby, in the accident. Not about the Woods. Not even about Danny. And I'm so tired. So very tired. What's happened to me, Scott? I don't like myself any more!'

And then to her horror she felt the sobs start shaking her body. Wretched, soul-destroying sobs from that so carefully hidden well of bitterness and agony deep within her.

Jodi felt warm, comforting arms come around her. Then her head was pressed into Scott's shoulder as he murmured, 'There, there, you poor girl. Whatever's been happening to you to bring you to this state?'

Then his arms picked up her shaking body against his firm one and he carried her into the lounge.

'You're just a featherweight,' his deep tones muttered as he put her down on the large sofa.

For a moment she missed the comforting closeness, and she tried desperately to stem her tears. Then a sense of relief swept through her as she felt him sit beside her and tuck her head back into his neck. A large hand smoothed her hair back soothingly.

Gradually the racking sobs died away, leaving her feeling thoroughly exhausted and ashamed. She felt a handkerchief dab effectively at her wet cheeks, and opened her eyes to gaze with blurred vision up into his face. She felt a sudden tension in the body she was leaning into. Reluctantly she stirred and reached for the damp handkerchief he proffered. She sat up, and then shivered as the warmth of his body left hers.

'It's getting chilly at night now,' he murmured, his gaze averted.

Silently he stood up as she attended to her face, and moved away to switch on and position a fan heater so that its warm air flowed over her. He straightened, and returned to her. But this time he sat not touching her, and stared down at the heater.

'Do you still classify someone as a stranger when you've cried all over them?' His soft voice was sombre.

Suddenly Jodi knew that ever since he had entered her bedroom this morning, only a few hours ago, she had not honestly been able to think of him as a stranger any longer. But she remained silent, twisting absently the damp piece of linen in her hands as she stared blindly down at them.

'And if you can become so upset by the thought that you don't seem to care any more, then you really must care quite a lot, don't you think?'

She raised her head sharply and looked speechlessly at him. He turned his head and returned her look. As her eyes locked with his, she thought for one fanciful moment that a small flame flickered deep within his dark eyes. Then he looked back at the heater on the floor.

'You've been under a great deal of stress. And, unless I'm way, way off the track, I think you have been for a long time. In fact, I don't believe you're merely suffering from stress. Things started getting on top of me last year and I did quite a bit of reading up on it all. Basically, stress is the response your body makes to any demand on it. It becomes bad when it's prolonged or too frequent. Stress comes from outside, causing you to either flee or fight. Mainly it causes physical changes like chronic tiredness, headaches, disturbed sleep.'

He looked up at her. She stared back at him silently, thinking about what she'd read and heard herself over the years, trying to take in what he was telling her.

'What is called "burnout" is a state of physical, emotional and mental exhaustion marked by——' He hesitated again, and then said gently, 'I believe you could have been almost burnt out, or at the very least well on the way towards it.'

She shook her head, starting to feel angry, but then a feeling of hopelessness began to sweep through her and she looked down at her clenched hands helplessly.

'I *am* a good listener, Jodi,' he murmured softly.

I could tell him, she knew suddenly. But her old fear of rejection kept her frozen.

When she still hadn't moved after a moment or so, he sighed and stood up. 'I'll bring you a drink.'

After he had disappeared, she let out a deep, quivering breath and relaxed back on the sofa with her eyes closed.

Images danced before her eyes of the cold, accusing

eyes of the director of nursing, of the furious, disappointed face of her father. Of Martin refusing to meet her eyes. And then, of course, more recently there was the wizened, wrinkled old-young, dark face of Danny. Always there was Danny. Danny with the bright, intelligent eyes. Trusting eyes that had changed to hopelessness. . .to. . .

She didn't realise Scott had returned, and had stood examining her white, quivering face for a few moments before he said gently, but very firmly, 'Jo, I want you to take these panadeine tablets with this mild sedative and go straight to bed. When you've had a sleep, and when you're ready, you and I are going to have a good talk.'

Her eyes flew open, and she automatically began to protest, but gave up when she saw the implacable expression on his face as he said, 'No more talking now; you're too exhausted.'

Reluctantly she swallowed the tablets he gave her, too exhausted to exert her independence any longer, even to ask what the small white tablet was.

As he helped her to her room with one strong arm around her waist, she wondered bleakly if she would have enough strength left to resist if he insisted on helping her into her nightie again. But he didn't. Only suddenly, he held her face between his two large hands and pressed his beautifully shaped lips firmly on hers, before turning wordlessly away.

After he had closed the door behind him, one shaking hand went up to her tingling lips. Two in one afternoon. And that had been no gentle, meant-to-comfort kiss. It had sought to convey a message to her.

She was almost asleep when she suddenly realised what that message could have been. Her eyes flew open. No matter what had happened to her, or what she had done, he cared about her. Impossible. He hardly knows me, she thought crossly, and angrily turned over in the bed. It was just her imagination. Then the medication took over, and before she could think it through she was asleep.

CHAPTER FIVE

THE sun was high in the sky again by the time Jodi had dressed and reluctantly left her room the next morning. She had slept soundly, but her eyes were still heavy, and she wondered a little angrily just how 'mild' that sedative had been. No more pills, she decided firmly, knowing how easy it could become relying on their help. Especially if those fits of grey depression kept returning.

This morning, she felt horribly embarrassed about her outburst and dreaded seeing Scott again. A tremendous sense of relief swept through her as she read the note under a fridge magnet.

'Out on patient rounds. Don't expect me until a late lunch.'

Just the kind of note he'd probably leave his wife one day.

The thought flashed through her mind, and a sharp pang immediately followed. He would be a very caring and thoughtful husband. She shook off the sudden wistfulness that touched her. It was absurd to feel jealous of some unknown woman. Better to occupy her mind in readiness for the 'talk' he had promised. Especially after letting her defences down so badly the previous night. She deliberately refused to think about what he had said about stress and burnout.

Goodness knew, she had certainly been under a tremendous amount of stress just lately. She had read once that not all stress was harmful. It set the adrenalin pumping and helped people to cope in the emergencies of life. But she also knew it had been estimated that about half of all visits to doctors were stress-related. But burnout? She had certainly heard about it, had even been warned about it in the IC course certificate, but had never done any in-depth study on it.

Jodi still had little appetite, but listlessly forced herself to have a cup of tea and some food, and then wandered outside into the garden. The amber tree was losing its leaves fast, and she scuffed through them to absorb the beauty of the bed of chrysanthemums. They were in a sheltered spot, but on closer inspection she saw that they were almost finished. She shivered in the cool breeze stirring the leaves. Winter wasn't very far away.

A screeching flock of pink and grey galahs landed in one of the tall gum trees. Then they must have sensed the intruder and took off again with more harsh screeching. The well looked after lawn sloped gently down to a barbed wire fence near the trees and she slowly made her way to look out over the paddocks stretching into the distance. Once again she couldn't help contrasting the patternwork of ploughed and green paddocks with the arid, bare paddocks of the area around that camp in Africa.

A tremor shook her, and then an overwhelming feeling of thankfulness that she was back in Australia. At the same time the kookaburra started up its harsh laughter. A slight smile flickered on her lips as she raised her head to look for it in the gently swaying branches above her. By the time she spotted it high in the gum tree it had stopped its challenge to the skies. In the sudden silence she heard a car approaching.

She stood still as the big Mercedes swung into the driveway. He had not seen her, and, taking a deep breath, she slowly made her way back to the house.

'Jodi!' she heard him bellow as she entered through the back door.

Before she could answer, he burst into the kitchen, and she stared at the look of relief that flooded his anxious face as he saw her in the doorway.

'For one moment, I thought——' He scowled ferociously and turned away, grabbed the electric kettle and made for the sink.

He had thought she had left! And been concerned. Even upset? For the first time in many long, dreary months, a faint song started up deep in Jodi. She had been right last night. He did care. He really cared. But would he still, if he knew all there was to know about her?

She stood rooted to the spot until he said gruffly over his shoulder, 'I left our lunch in the hallway. You collect it while I get out some plates.'

This time Jodi obeyed without even an inner protest that he was throwing orders around again. On a small table just inside the front entrance were two plastic bags. When she picked them up, the unmistakable smell of cooked chicken made her realise she was actually hungry for a change. The other held what looked like a freshly cut lettuce and some large, out-of-season red tomatoes.

'My last patient has his own hothouse. And I didn't have the heart to tell Mrs Miller we'd had chicken for lunch yesterday,' Scott said casually as she carried them over to the sink. And just as casually he added, 'I was very relieved you were sleeping so well last night the few times I checked you.'

Her eyes flew to his averted face. He had checked on her a 'few' times? She felt heat stealing over her at the thought of him watching her as she slept.

'After we've had something to eat, we'll go find your brother's house. I'm pretty sure I know where it is. Mrs Dunne was also a mine of information.'

Jodi suddenly felt a great sense of relief that he had apparently changed his mind about having the threatened talk. Or had he just postponed it?

'Did. . .?' Jodi cleared her husky throat and tried again, desperately trying to sound as casual and unconcerned as Scott. 'Did she know who was looking after David and Ann's animals?'

'Yes.' This time, Scott's voice was abrupt. 'Apparently Bill Wood was.'

Jodi stared at him. Their eyes clashed for a moment, and she was the first to look away. His had looked so angry for a moment. She wasn't quite game to ask what he was annoyed about now.

'How are they today?' she murmured.

'Their son rang me earlier and said they were doing very well. Bill's being carefully monitored still, but Vera's expected to be out of Intensive Care in a couple of days if everything goes well.'

It was not a silent or uncomfortable atmosphere while they had lunch, mainly due to the smooth flow of conversation about the area and its local identities initiated by Scott. In fact, Jodi had relaxed considerably by the time they had rinsed the few dishes they had used.

But that changed immediately as she was hanging up her damp tea-towel and said, 'I won't be long. It'll only take me a few minutes to re-pack my bag and——'

'No.' Scott's tone of voice was calm but definite.

'You aren't taking your case. We're just going to find your brother's place and then come straight back here.'

Jodi swung round angrily. 'I can't stay here!'

'And why not?'

She opened her mouth, and then closed it with a snap. Scott put his hands on his hips and studied her angry face steadily.

'I don't need a reason!' she said through gritted teeth. 'And you would have to be one of the bossiest men of any I've ever had the misfortune to meet! You'd certainly give my father a run for his money!'

That indefinable light flashed again into his eyes as he continued to stare at her. Then suddenly his lips twitched and amusement lit his face as he grinned at her.

'You'd better believe it! According to my dear aunt Edith I *am* the bossiest. Especially with pigheaded females.'

Pigheaded? Why. . .why. . .?

Jodi fought for control. And lost. 'And I've had considerable practice dealing with impossible doctors with self-inflated egos who consider themselves little gods!'

She turned on her heel, more determined than ever to pack. His roar of laughter stopped her dead.

'So. . .so have I. Had plenty of practice. . .' he gasped between gusts of laughter as he stared at the furious face she presented to him. 'Oh, Jodi, how I wish you'd been there to help me! We'd have been an unbeatable team!'

She stared at him. Mesmerised. He was so incredibly handsome. Even that thick dark hair seemed to vibrate with life as he stared back at her with the laughter filling his face gradually fading.

'I'm still trying to work out whether your huge eyes are really green or not. And when you're angry, you are very, very beautiful,' he murmured very softly.

Beautiful? He thought she was beautiful?

Their eyes locked. In a dream, she vaguely realised he had moved closer. Then she felt his arms around her. And knew that that was what she had been waiting for all morning.

This time there was no comfort in them, only a sense of urgency. His lips on hers were no longer a stranger's. She felt her own body springing to life, curving closer to his firm one as though it had known him a long time. He moved his legs, and suddenly she was cradled between his thighs, leaning against him helplessly, her body seeking his even more intimately.

He gave a slight groan as his lips at last released hers, and began to trail a path of fire down her neck.

'So full of fire and passion,' Jodi heard him murmur as though from a distance. And then he moved, and his heat left hers. 'But I think that had better be all. For now, at least.'

Her dazed eyes focused on his again as he backed away from her. Never before had she not been the first one to draw back from a man. And those few occasions over the years when she had felt her own passion and desire begin to burn had always made her back off. And back off fast.

She was still staring at him, feeling bereft and foolishly, incredibly hurt, when he reached the doorway and stopped.

'You'll need a warmer jumper. And don't be long. We still have to have that talk I promised you, and surgery today is earlier than yesterday.' He paused and looked sternly and directly at her. 'And if you dare carry out that monstrously heavy case, I'll leave it dumped in the driveway.' Then he disappeared.

It was a full minute before Jodi stirred. Then she began to tremble, that insidious ache developing behind her eyes again. More than ever now, she couldn't stay. Even if he did do what he had just said. She deliberately fanned the embers of her anger. How dared he? Dump her case, would he?

And he would too, the impossible man, she fumed as she haphazardly packed her case. Especially if he were true to form. She had only taken out a few essential items, so it didn't take very long before she had finished collecting her things. And what did it matter if she did leave something behind?

She furiously grabbed an old jumper before closing the case, and stormed back outside more slowly than she would have liked with it in her hand. He had been right. It was too heavy for her. But nothing would make her admit it. She had more reason than ever to get away now. And if he did carry out his threat, even if it cost the earth, there were such things as taxis, weren't there?

The breeze had strengthened into a cold wind from the west. She caught the full brunt of it as she opened the front door. Dropping the case on the veranda, she started to pull on the hand-knitted jumper. It was only then that she realised it was the ghastly pale pink one she hated. It had always made her look insipid, even more so since she had lost weight and her face had lost its colour. In fact, she thought it had been one of the battered pieces of clothing that had been left behind at the village.

She paused briefly, and then savagely finished hauling it on over her head. It had shrunk disastrously with repeated washings and fitted her snugly, despite her loss of weight.

As she reached down to pick up the case, she heard heavy footsteps slowly start up the front steps. She froze, and then straightened, staring defiantly at Scott as he reached her.

His eyes darkened as they travelled over her body, and she became even more conscious of the tightness of the jumper. Obviously, he wasn't concerned one scrap about its colour. Suddenly she realised just how it clung to the shape of her breasts.

Then her eyes locked with his. This time, he hurriedly looked away. But not before she had seen the flame leap into his eyes. Her heart leapt. Had that been desire—for her, Jodi Banner? Perhaps he hadn't been rejecting her before.

'Jodi, you really shouldn't be by yourself for a while yet,' he said a little too rapidly. He brought his gaze back to her face. This time only concern was revealed there. His voice softened coaxingly as he added, 'You know you aren't well enough.'

'I know nothing of the sort,' she said haughtily, 'and if you won't take me I'll find other transport.' She paused, and, despite all her efforts, lost a little of her poise as Scott continued to stare at her. 'You've just given me even more reason not to stay,' she snapped.

He scowled angrily, and she continued defiantly, 'I suppose there are such things as taxis. Even if they take forever to get here from Toowoomba.'

They both stared stubbornly at each other for a long minute. His expression softened subtly.

'Is it my desires or your own you don't trust?' he murmured in a husky voice.

Jodi felt the tide of red flood her face, and then

sudden fear made her take a step back. Not fear of Scott, she acknowledged numbly. Fear of that foreign, responsive stab of fire deep within her.

Sudden regret replaced the gleam of mockery in Scott's face. 'But my putting pressure on you is only adding to your stress levels, I suppose.' He shrugged. 'Oh, all right, you stubborn female! Be it on your own head!' But he was scowling again as he reached for her case.

She felt weak in the legs with relief at his sudden capitulation. He had opened the passenger door for her, and was throwing her case in the boot before she was sure she had the strength to move.

After she had climbed into the luxurious car, she slammed the door viciously, angry with herself as much as with him.

In the process of seating himself, Scott winced. Despite the sudden hint of laughter in his voice, he said mournfully, 'The poor car. Don't you like it?'

Jodi refused to acknowledge the pang of regret that flashed through her. 'No, I don't,' she snapped. 'It's ostentatious.'

He chuckled softly, but remained silent as he backed the car down the driveway.

'My father has one the same,' Jodi blurted out.

There was silence for a moment. Jodi stared blindly through the windscreen, already regretting her burst of temper.

'And is that a reason not to like white Mercedes?' Scott asked softly at last.

She couldn't answer him.

He waited a moment, and then said conversationally, 'What does your father do? Is he an accountant like David?'

Jodi gave a derisive snort. 'Nothing so lowly. He's a doctor. Not just any old doctor, mind you. He's a very prestigious surgeon. And just for the record, his car's black!'

'Uh-oh! I don't think I like the sound of all that,' Scott said teasingly after another brief pause. 'Don't you like your brother being an accountant?'

'*I* think it's a marvellous profession. Father doesn't,' Jodi said shortly.

'I see,' he said thoughtfully. And suddenly Jodi knew what he was thinking, even as he continued. 'He wanted his son to follow in his footsteps. What about his daughter?'

It was Jodi's turn to be silent. Then she stirred and said reluctantly, 'He put even more pressure on me when I was in high school than he ever did on David. But I never reached the tertiary scholastic level to get into med school. He wanted me to go back and repeat the Higher School Certificate until I did.'

'And you wouldn't.'

'No.'

Jodi thought drearily of the many times she had listened to her father's well thought out arguments that January after the results had come out. That had soon ceased, to be replaced by his furious, autocratic demands that she 'do as she was told!'

She had only been seventeen, and had so nearly given in. After all, she had only missed out by a couple of points. But she had never really wanted to be a doctor anyway. Nursing had always appealed to her as a better opportunity to have more in-depth involvement with people. But it had only been the memory of how frustrated her mother had been trying to care for two children, and keep up with her career as a doctor to the level to satisfy her husband's high expectations, that had in the end stopped her.

Suddenly she found herself telling Scott about those tense weeks, her feeling of failure. It had been the first time she had gone against her father's wishes since her mother had died a couple of years before.

'He still hasn't given up on me even after all this time,' she added grimly. 'And still hasn't forgiven me —or David, for that matter.' Jodi couldn't help the trace of bitterness that still lingered creeping into her voice. 'Even when I topped my year academically, he didn't even bother to turn up at the graduation.'

Scott gave an unexpected snort. 'You were lucky. My whole tribe turned up—aunts, uncles, cousins, as well as Mum. We were only allowed two seat tickets, but they just ignored that. I'm still not sure how they all managed to get admitted. Only I don't think I've ever felt as embarrassed in my life!'

A stab of envy struck Jodi. 'It must be nice having such a large family,' she said softly.

Scott was silent for a moment. Then he sounded a little grim when he said, 'Not all the time, that's for sure. Especially when they gang up on you.'

Jodi looked at him curiously, and then plucked up the courage to ask bluntly, 'Why did you leave your job and take this one, Scott? And where were you a registrar?'

He told her the name of a large, well-known hospital in Sydney, and then said quietly, 'I needed a change. Ever since graduating, I've thought being a GP would suit me. But in a large city practice somewhere.' He was silent for a moment, then he said with a trace of self-disgust, 'Unlike you, I let another person dictate to me what area of medicine to go into.'

He was silent for a while, and then Jodi wasn't quite sure just how serious he was when he added with a wry grin, 'It's one of the penalties of being a member of my family that I now find myself doing locum work on the Darling Downs in Queensland for at least twelve months.' He thought for a moment and then said slowly, 'Strangely enough, though, yesterday I was really pleased to get back here from Sydney. It felt like I'd come home.'

They both fell silent. Jodi suddenly longed to know, even more than she had yesterday, who could have had such a powerful influence on this strong man to make him take a course he had not been entirely happy about. An unexpected pang caught her unawares at the thought of Scott caring about a woman enough to let her influence him so much. She continued to muse in silence, watching the farmlands speed past.

They were travelling in the opposite direction they had taken to Toowoomba. A few kilometres from Wingeen, the large properties had given way to smaller subdivisions of only a few acres. Houses of brick or weatherboard of all sizes dotted the landscape amid naturally tree-studded surroundings or carefully landscaped gardens.

'This conversion of large farms into smaller acreages and the resulting increase in population out here are the main reasons the community decided they now need their own health facilities.'

Scott slowed down and pointed to several homes where he had patients.

'It rather surprised me just how many families found it very hard to get used to not having the doctor or the chemist around the corner. Most are trying to fulfil their dreams of living out in the bush not too far from a city where they can get work, and they find the reality quite different from their expectations. The children come, or one or both of their parents can no longer cope by themselves, and move in. When illness especially occurs, transport often becomes a problem. Those with good paying jobs usually manage to have two vehicles. But it often happens that, with a chronically ill member of the family to cope with, health expenses make it difficult to afford the two cars. Hence the district nursing was started.'

Jodi tensed. She opened her mouth to make a tart retort about the African bush people's difficulties in getting the most basic health care making the poorest out here look very luxurious indeed. Before she could speak, however, the mobile telephone rang.

Scott slowed the car as he reached for it.

'It's Margaret Field here. You in the car, Dr Scott?'

'Yes, Margaret. I'm not far from your place, in fact. How's Beth?'

'She didn't go to school today. And she's refusing to try and eat again.'

Jodi saw Scott's face tighten as he said crisply, 'Want me to pop in and see her?'

Relief rang over the air waves as the woman said a little tearfully, 'Oh, could you? I know her check-up isn't until next week. I'd bring her to the surgery this evening, but the baby's had a bad cold, and——'

'No problem, Margaret,' Scott's voice softened. 'I'll be there in a few minutes.'

Jodi's heart sank as he glanced at her after replacing the phone.

'Sorry,' he said briefly, 'This shouldn't take long. That poor devil of a mother needs all the support she can get.' At her enquiring look, he added curtly, 'Cystic fibrosis.'

Jodi drew a deep breath. Years ago she had worked for several months in a children's ward, and her heart had always gone out to the children and families of those with that wretched condition. Few cystic fibrosis sufferers reached their twenties, although constant research was always bringing hope that one day a breakthrough would increase their life expectancy.

'Beth is one of the patients Edith used to visit at least once a day. Mainly postural drainage on the chest, keeping an eye on her diet, and giving Margaret support,' he added significantly as Jodi looked across at him.

Her heart sank even further. He was still expecting her to consider his offer of the job.

She resented him even more when they had been at the Fields' place for only a few minutes. The strained, exhausted face of the mother was bad enough. Then the pale, thin little girl with a beaming smile for Scott, but quite breathless, tore at her heart-strings. She was beautiful. And it wasn't just her lovely black curls and daintily shaped features. It was a beauty from within that shone forth.

Where yesterday Jodi's emotions had seemed to be on hold when with patients, now they were being tugged far too strongly.

'This ya girlfriend, Doc?' Beth asked slowly, grinning cheekily at Jodi.

'Heavens, no,' Jodi flashed a little too vehemently before Scott could respond. 'Who'd have this bossy thing for a boyfriend?'

Then she could have bitten her tongue as she felt the blush creeping into her cheeks and Margaret

Field looked sharply from her to Scott.

'This is Sister Jodi,' Scott punished her immediately by saying. 'She's David Banner's sister, and she's a very good nurse.'

She flashed him an angry glance, but before she could respond Margaret gave her a beaming smile and said, 'Oh, are you the lady who saved Bill Wood's life?'

'Me? N-not really,' stammered Jodi in some confusion, feeling as though her face was really on fire now. 'I just happened to be standing next to him when he. . . But how did you know?' she asked with a frown.

Scott gave a chuckle. 'This might be a scattered community, but word travels fast among my patients. And everyone knows the Woods.'

'Yes,' said Margaret brightly, 'all this land was once part of their original farm. Apparently owned by the family for several generations.'

It was obvious she was ready to go on about the history of the place, and Jodi was glad when Scott said swiftly, 'you'll have to visit Margaret and Beth one day and let them tell you all about it. But now, young lady,' he said firmly, turning to Beth, 'what have you been up to?'

The smiles of mother and daughter disappeared.

'She hasn't been eating properly again,' said Margaret with a worried frown.

'I'm too. . .too short of breath and all that muck's there again,' Beth scowled at her mother. 'Mum doesn't thump me enough sometimes to shift it properly. I wish Sister Edith would hurry up and come back!'

Jodi avoided Scott's eyes as he moved to run his stethoscope over the thin little chest and then percuss it. She knew that it usually wouldn't only be the mucus in her lungs that made it difficult for Beth to eat. CF was a multi-system disorder. The right high-protein, high-calorie, low-fat diet was so very important. She wondered if Beth was on pancreatic enzyme treatment as well.

'Hmm,' Scott said after a thorough examination. 'Afraid she's right, Margaret. The mucus has built up too much. She needs more postural drainage.'

'But I just don't know how I'm going to give her more time,' Margaret said with a choked voice. 'The baby's been keeping me up at night with teething, and after five minutes thumping Beth's back I feel my hands are going to fall off. And so many times a day. . .'

Jodi clenched her hands behind her back, wondering where the father was. Didn't he help out? She knew how very important it was to give a few periods each day of such therapy to cystic fibrosis patients. The cause of the disease was still unknown, but the formation of thick mucous throughout the body causing obstructions in many organs was one of its characteristics. Pulmonary complications such as bronchopneumonia and chronic bronchitis was common. It was vital to care for the lungs properly. The build-up of mucus there made infections occur far too frequently.

'Do you still have a repeat prescription left on the antibiotics?'

When Margaret shook her head silently at Scott, Jodi saw that she wasn't far from tears. Defeat seemed in every drooping, weary inch of her.

'Well,' he said briskly, 'I'll thump your back for Mum this time, young lady, and then write another prescription out.'

'Would it. . .would it be OK if I gave you the postural drainage, Beth?' Jodi heard her voice say shakily. She saw the surprise on Scott's face as he looked sharply across at her, and added defensively, 'I did quite a bit of it a long time ago, so I don't know how good I'll be or how long I'll be able to do it for. But. . . but I can give it a go while you write the script.'

'That's an excellent idea, Sis,' Beth grimaced at her knowingly. 'And that'll give the doc and Mum a chance to have one of their talks about me.'

Scott hesitated for a moment, and then said slowly, 'I don't want you to tire yourself out too, much, Jodi. You may not believe it, but I really didn't bring you here for that.'

She cocked one eyebrow resignedly at him. He stared back steadily, and then he nodded abruptly. 'Right, Beth, into your room with you.'

As Jodi followed the little girl slowly, she was already regretting her impulsive offer. It had never been something she had enjoyed doing. It was part of the physiotherapists' task in hospital, and she had always welcomed them back with relief after she had been forced to do it when they were off duty.

Ten minutes later, she was feeling even sorrier for herself. Her hands and wrists were aching from the unaccustomed thumping. And she wondered again, as she had many times in the past, how the carers of cystic fibrous children managed this day after day, year after year.

Beth was exhausted too when they had finished. Jodi had always been a real sucker for sick kids who could still come up with a smile. Her heart softened as Beth grinned a little crookedly up at her from where she still lay face down, with her little body over a couple of pillows to give the lungs better drainage.

'Th-thanks. . .' she gasped, 'Better. . .'

Jodi gave her a wave as she retreated, 'You're welcome, love,' she said softly, and backed into a solid form.

'Oops,' said Scott's voice in her ear as she felt both hands grasp her waist. 'All finished? Sorry I was so long.' He looked gravely at her before turning to Beth. 'I'll call in tomorrow, sweetheart,' he said gently.

A thin white arm gave him a slight wave, and then she turned her head away. Scott stared across the room for a moment, and then Jodi heard the soft sigh he gave as he released her and turned away.

'We'd better get you over to your brother's, before I get any more calls,' he said abruptly.

Even when they had waved goodbye to a slightly happier Margaret, and were bumping down the rough track to the road again, Jodi could still feel the heat on her waist where his fingers had absently caressed her while he had looked with that helpless, weary look at his little patient.

CHAPTER SIX

'DOES Beth's father help with her?' Jodi ventured at last, when Scott remained silent as they turned on to the main country road again.

'That's part of the whole sorry mess,' Scott snorted angrily. 'He walked out on them all a couple of weeks ago. Just said he couldn't take it any more.'

'Oh, poor Margaret!' Jodi exclaimed.

From her experiences in the past, Jodi knew that illness for such a long time in families often caused very serious breakdowns of marriages, when one partner crumpled under the never-ending stress.

She looked across at Scott's grim face. *He'd* never walk out, she thought suddenly. And then wondered why she was so sure of that. She looked quickly away, aware that she was examining him too closely.

Why would he never walk out?

Because he cares very deeply for people, came the answer. And he has that special, added strength that comes from a deep inner faith.

The ensuing silence between them was a comfortable one, both engrossed in their thoughts. But it was only a few minutes later that Scott slowed the car.

'A bit further on, this road comes out on the busy Warrego highway, which runs for hundreds of kilometres from Toowoomba west to the outback, and if I'm right. . . Ah, yes! On the mailbox there—Banner,' Scott said triumphantly.

It was a large, single-storeyed, cream brick house set

well back from the road, surrounded by a beautifully landscaped garden. Instead of tiles it had a corrugated metal roof that glinted in the sunlight.

'Oh,' said Jodi softly as the car moved slowly down the long driveway to stop near the front entrance. 'It's beautiful.'

'About twenty acres, I'd say,' said Scott as he looked across the few small fenced areas. 'Quite a big block for this area. But, as I feared, that must be your nearest neighbour's roof just showing over that rise. Must be at least two kilometres away.'

Jodi chose to ignore the concern in his voice and scrambled from the car. 'David told me they'd put in a salt-water pool,' she said eagerly, and led the way along a path towards the rear of the house.

Scott whistled at the sight of the beautifully shaped, large pool. 'Glad they've had the sense to put up that high safety fence,' he murmured, 'and those large tanks.' At Jodi's look of enquiry, he added, 'For rain-water storage. No town supply right out here yet.'

The pool area contained beautiful shrubbery and a paved area in front of a small garden shed.

'They probably have locked away lovely outdoor furniture in there,' mused Scott as he pointed to the shed. 'To go with that gorgeous barbecue.'

It was very peaceful. Jodi took a deep breath and looked around with sheer delight. And then suddenly she gave a gurgle of laughter.

'Well! They told me about Buttercup, but not about those goats! I wonder who milks them all?'

She swung round to Scott, her face alight with the thought of her diminutive sister-in-law having to look after, even milk the half-dozen goats that were grazing in a nearby paddock.

Scott was staring at her with a peculiar look on his face. 'That's the first time I've seen you smile.'

She watched with fascination as his throat moved and he swallowed rapidly. His voice was even softer and huskier as he added, 'You should do it all the time. You're even more beautiful when you do, Jodi.'

The sun was shining on the raven sheen of his hair. That smile started up in his eyes again, and she was still waiting for the appearance of that elusive dimple, when she realised he had moved closer. She was still staring spellbound at him as his arms reached out and grasped her above the elbows.

Then suddenly she wrenched herself away. 'No,' she managed harshly, 'I don't want you to touch me again.' She turned her back on him and stomped towards the back door which David had given her the key for.

'Now that was a lie, if ever I've heard one,' Scott said matter-of-factly.

He was close behind her, and suddenly she wished she could run into the house and slam the door in his face.

'I don't lie,' she threw angrily over her shoulder as her trembling fingers refused to fit the key in the lock.

His large hand reached over and steadied hers so that they turned the key together. 'What's even worse,' he whispered loudly in her ear in his deep voice, 'you believe your own lies.'

She bit her lip, and pushed the door open. He followed her through the laundry-room and into a large, country-styled kitchen. While she looked around curiously, he strode confidently past her and disappeared. Relieved to be alone, she set about exploring the kitchen and its contents. The cupboards and freezer were well-stocked. She was immensely relieved to know that she would be able to cope very well in that regard.

Then Scott returned with her case. 'Where do you want this?' he asked hurriedly. 'I've had a call out to a patient. Can you manage now?'

She nodded briefly. He stared at her, and then said in even tones, 'Will you promise faithfully to ring me if you need anything?'

She nodded again. 'I do need to be alone for a while, Scott,' she assured him in a low voice.

He looked at her steadily, and then turned back to the front hallway. Stopping near the phone, he scribbled on the pad beside it.

'My number,' he said briefly, and then looked up at her. 'And I haven't thanked you for helping Beth, Jodi,' he said softly.

This time his lips touched her forehead briefly, and then he was gone.

Her forehead felt branded as Jodi watched the large white car disappear. Her emotions were in turmoil. She had found herself unconsciously waiting for his beautifully shaped mouth to touch her lips again as he had leaned towards her, and felt horribly disappointed when they had not.

She shrugged, disgusted with herself. She had been so abrupt with Scott before that she would not really have been surprised if he had merely left her case in the driveway and taken off!

She took a deep breath. As the sound of his car faded, she was suddenly very aware of the silence. She hurriedly closed the front door. Solitude was what she had been desperately longing for, she told herself firmly.

And she was still telling herself that the following

evening as she sat in the large kitchen eating her solitary meal.

To her relief, the evening before a quiet teenage boy had arrived and drawled briefly that Doc had organised him to milk the cow. She'd wondered briefly who had been doing it since Bill Wood. Then she had thought of something else.

'What. . .what about the goats? Do they need milking too?'

He had grinned a little. 'Naw, none milkin' yet. Won't be long, though, till a couple have their kids.'

She had smiled weakly back at him, but been too tired even to bother to go and watch him milk. Later he had knocked on the door and handed her more than half a bucket of creamy milk which she had looked at with some dismay. Taking only a jugful, she had insisted he take the rest. She supposed he had returned again since, but if so he had not disturbed her again.

Sleep had been a long time coming, but then had been deep and dreamless. In fact, she had once again slept very late. The rest of the day had been spent resting and walking short distances over the gently sloping paddocks, and exploring the garden that her brother had written to her briefly about establishing from scratch. She pulled a few weeds, wondering wistfully when she'd ever have her own garden, an ambition that had been dormant for years now.

At first she had thoroughly enjoyed being alone. She had shrugged off the sudden regret that had touched her when she was eating lunch by herself, thinking of the meals she had shared with Scott in the brief time since they had met.

Perhaps it was because she had been so constantly on the go for so long, but, whatever the reason, by the time the sun had lit the dark clouds on the western horizon with awesome colours she had almost given up refusing to admit she was rapidly becoming bored with her own company.

'Impossible!' she muttered angrily. 'I couldn't possibly be bored in one day!'

When darkness had settled over the paddocks again, she became even more edgy. She had only ever lived in a city before her time in Africa. Even in the camp, there had been the cooking fires to give some light, people moving about. Tonight, it was pitch-black. Low cloud had cut off the light of the stars. Even the animals had settled for the night, and the silence seemed intense. She had never realised before how dark it could be right away from the city.

After she had finished eating, she pulled shut the curtains on the large picture windows in the living area, and turned on a few more lights. She tried to watch television, but weariness drove her at last very early to bed. For the first time in her life, she was tempted to leave the lights on, but, exasperated with herself, she switched them all off. She hesitated over her bed light, thought briefly of her brother's electricity bill, but left it on.

Still, tired as she was, she couldn't settle. All day she had refused to dwell on the doctor who had helped her. In the darkness, she at last admitted unwillingly that she had been waiting for him to contact her all day.

At least he could have phoned, she thought crossly as she tried to put him out of her mind. But images of Scott kept slipping into her head, try as she might to dismiss them. In the end, angry with herself, she flicked off the light, and, after tossing and turning a while longer, did eventually go to sleep.

Jodi had been dreaming. Unpleasant dreams. Frightening dreams. She wasn't sure what woke her. Whatever it was sent her bolt upright.

Then she heard a sharp, echoing crack. Still half asleep, for one dreadful moment she was back in the camp, and instinctively flung herself on to the floor, lying flat and still, every sense straining to hear. All was silent, and she had started to relax, calling herself all kinds of an idiot, when the sound came again. This time there was a loud ping after the noise, as though a bullet had ricocheted off metal.

Wide awake now, Jodi froze in horror. It had only been a little more than a week since she had heard that sound in the middle of the night. A terrified moan escaped her lips as she stared into the darkness towards the window. Then she tried to pull herself together. This was Australia, for goodness' sake. This was a quiet country house. There were no guerrillas, no rival clans after the supplies of food.

She must be mistaken. Who on earth would be shooting off a gun here?

As she strained to hear, she realised there was a faint light coming through her curtained windows. She waited for what seemed like forever. Then she crawled across the floor and carefully peeped outside.

The clouds had lifted, and a full moon had risen. It was quite bright outside. There was a movement down near the pool. Two dark figures appeared briefly. She thought she heard one of them laugh, and then watched with horror as they paused. Then a much louder shot rang out.

Afterwards, she never quite knew how she crawled her way from the bedroom into the hallway to the phone, terrified that the intruders would see movement in the house. She found the slip of paper but had to carry it over to a window to make out the numbers. Trembling fingers at last dialled and she seemed to wait forever. Then Scott's voice was there. For a moment she couldn't speak.

'Hello? Who is it, please?' His voice had sharpened.

'Scott. . .' she managed.

There was a very brief silence and then he said urgently, 'Jodi? Is that you?'

'Oh, Scott,' she suddenly wailed, 'I'm so frightened. . . I. . .'

'What is it?'

'Two. . . Two men. . .outside.'

She heard his sharp indrawn breath and then, 'Are all your doors looked?' he said sharply.

Sudden uncertainty gripped her. Had she locked the back door when she had come in that last time?

'I. . .I'm not sure!' she wailed again.

'Check the doors and stay away from the windows. I'll be right there!'

'But Scott. . .they've got guns,' she choked out, but then realised the phone was dead. 'Oh, no. . .no. . .'

Desperately she tried to pull herself together. He hadn't heard her. If Scott came, they might. . . might. . .

The thought of anything happening to him sent her stumbling back to her bedroom and peering out of her window. A few clouds had drifted across the moon and it was only shadows where she had seen the two dark figures. She didn't know how long she stood frozen at the window. Then she remembered the door. With a gasp she fled on shaking legs.

As she entered the laundry-room, two things happened simultaneously. She saw the door start swinging open and outside there was a sudden burst of shouting mingled with raucous laughter and another couple of shots. For a split-second she froze at a loud cry of pain from outside.

The person pushing open the door also paused, but then a large hand appeared around the door and it started to open further.

Jodi gasped and launched herself at the door. It slammed on the hand, but didn't close. There was a muffled groan of pain. Jodi gritted her teeth and leaned harder against it. Someone yelled.

Then Jodi heard a noise that she had never wanted to hear again—the terrified cries of children. Her breath was coming in short gasps as she reeled away from the door.

'No. . .no. . . Danny. . .' she panted.

Then the door was flung open violently.

'Jodi!' a voice roared. 'It's me, Scott!'

'Scott! Oh, Scott, they're hurting the children,' she screamed, and flew towards him.

'Children! What children? It's me that's hurting. You slammed the door on my hand!' He was bent over the laundry tub, turning on the tap as he spoke, and she saw with horror the blood dripping from his hand.

She joined him on shaking legs, suddenly realising that the sound had died down outside. Then there was a couple of loud bleeting sounds.

'There it is again. . .' she started to whisper, and then listened again.

'That was the goats,' said Scott through gritted teeth. 'Your companions were enjoying chasing them!'

'Goats,' she said faintly, a wave of dizziness hitting her. She reached to steady herself, and grasped hold of Scott.

'Before you faint, do you think you could get me some ice for this hand?' his voice snarled at her.

'I. . .I'll. . .yes. . .' she muttered through numb lips.

They were both still as the wail of a distant siren reached them.

'I phoned the police,' he bit off, 'but I doubt if our friends will wait around to welcome them. Now, do you think. . .?'

'Yes. . .yes. . .' she muttered distractedly and fled to grab an ice-cube tray and her brother's first-aid kit.

In a haze, somehow she emptied the ice into a plastic bag, and while he held it to his hand went to see what her brother kept in the way of first-aid equipment.

'Let. . .let me put some of this disinfectant over that cut. . .' she managed faintly when she returned.

He lifted the ice while she applied a pad where the skin was broken. Already his four fingers were swollen. Her fingers were trembling badly as she pulled open a crêpe bandage and began to bandage over the pad. She heard him catch his breath in pain, and another wave of dizziness swept over her. She fought it off for a moment, then felt the roll of bandage slip out of her hand. She lifted her head with difficulty to the grim face above her, and felt her lips begin to move sluggishly.

'I'm sorry. . .I think I'm going to. . .' She saw his expression change just as his face moved to a crazy angle, and then a grey mist began to descend.

'Oh, no, you don't!' Scott's voice roared above her.

A firm hand grabbed her as she slumped forward, and eased her down to the cold, tiled floor. Then her head was pressed down between her legs.

That savage voice snarled again, 'You can't faint

now! It sounds as if someone's hurt out there. You've got to help me! Especially since you've busted my hand!'

Unfeeling brute.

She started to raise her head indignantly, and then closed her eyes as the room swung round again. The hand on her head pushed harder.

'Stay there. Just a moment longer.'

There was a peal of a bell and then a loud pounding on the front door. For a moment, Jodi thought it was just the throb in her head and then the hand was removed abruptly.

'It's the police,' Scott's voice said hurriedly. 'I'll be back in a moment.'

When he reappeared, a very large, burly policeman was with him. Jodi had dragged herself upright, and stared at them helplessly.

'I thought I told you to stay put,' snapped Scott.

'You also said you needed help,' she said shakily, and then raised her chin stubbornly. 'I've never fainted in my life!'

'Just as well. There's a stupid idiot of a kid out there who sure needs someone's help,' the officer said impatiently. 'Bloke's been shot. My offsider's with him. Other idiot's taken off, so if you could take over out there, Doc, I'll see if I can grab him.'

Scott hesitated for a moment as he surveyed Jodi, then he snapped again, 'You'd better get something warmer on before you come out.'

Jodi glanced down at herself, only then aware of her sole item of clothing. Her warm winter nightie had a plunging neckline. With an incoherent murmur she pulled the edges together and made for the bedroom as fast as her shaking legs would allow.

She went to snatch up her long woollen dressing-gown, and then paused. Goodness knew what faced her outside. She forced herself not to remember what a gunshot wound could be like, and quickly pulled on a fleecy-lined tracksuit with trembling hands.

A young, scared face peered up at her from the ground as she joined the men crouched beside him. A large spotlight from the patrol car lit the area reasonably well.

'We put a tourniquet on his leg,' the big man beside Scott was saying abruptly. 'Bullet must've hit an artery below the knee.'

'The bleeding's slowed down now,' a younger policeman said with relief as he turned to inspect Jodi.

'Why have you taken so long——?' Scott began to snarl as Jodi crouched down beside him, and then stopped abruptly as he took in the fact that she was dressed. He glanced up at the other men. 'Could one of you get my gear out of my car?' he said grimly. 'I parked it back up the road a bit.' He rattled off a few instructions, and then returned his attention to the still groaning youth.

'So that's why I didn't know you were here,' Jodi murmured shakily. 'You had the phone switched over to the car still. I didn't dream you could be here so fast.'

He glanced up again sharply from examining the youth's leg. Dark eyes searched her white face intently, and then emotion suddenly twisted his features. He looked away quickly, but not before warmth swept through Jodi as she saw the extent of his concern for her.

'I was already on my way to see you when you phoned,' he said in a low voice, 'It's so early, I didn't think of you already being in bed!' Then he added with a catch in his voice, 'I'll always be grateful I was so close.'

'You. . .you. . .so will I,' murmured Jodi shakily, and then added in an attempt to wipe out the look on his face, 'But I bet your poor hand isn't glad.'

She was relieved to see his face relax a little. He stood up as he said abruptly, 'It certainly still hurts like the devil. You'll have to do most of the work here, I'm afraid.'

'As there doesn't seem much point in chasing after that other young fool now the clouds have come over again,' the policeman said grimly, 'I may as well stay and help, too.'

The bullet had sliced along the calf muscle a few inches below the back of the knee, then ploughed through a deeper layer before speeding on its way. They tried putting a pressure pad over the short gash and the exit wound on the outer side of the leg, but when the tourniquet was slowly released the blood seeped through rapidly again.

'There's no help for it,' Scott said briskly after tightening the tourniquet again. 'I don't think it's hit a main tibial artery, but we'll have to try and get to the blood vessels. Ever done any suturing?' he shot at Jodi.

She stared in horror at him.

'Well? Have you?'

'Suturing? So. . .so much, I'd hoped never to have to do any again,' she managed through dry lips at last.

An arrested look flashed into his eyes, but he said commandingly, 'As I'm out of action, you have to.'

He stared at her a moment longer, and then turned to the constable. 'We can't leave that tourniquet on so tightly for the length of time it'll take to get him to hospital, or even my surgery. And he's lost enough blood now. I carry an emergency pack in the car sufficient to do the repair work, but we'll have to get him inside.'

They immobilised the leg with a rough splint hastily prepared by one of the constables, and before long the now thoroughly terrified young man was stretched out on Jodi's bed, which she'd hastily covered with a protective sheet of plastic.

'We. . .we was only having a bit of harmless target practice,' he whined to the unsympathetic policeman.

'Harmless! Scaring Sister here almost out of her wits? Shooting up defenceless goats? *And* shooting yourself!' queried one of them sarcastically. 'By the size of that hole, you must've been using a big rifle, too.'

'It was the other bloke's. His dad's old 303. The. . . the bullet must've hit something and spun sideways,' the injured man muttered. 'Hurtin' like blazes.'

'Oh, no!' Jodi swung around in distress. 'Are any of the goats hurt?'

'My mate's checking them out now,' she was assured.

'All ready, Jodi,' Scott said impatiently, 'let's get on with it.'

They had both washed their hands thoroughly and donned sterile gloves from the pack that she had carefully opened beforehand on the swiftly cleared bedside table. Without thinking about it, Jodi grabbed a second pair and carefully eased them on over the first. She glanced up and saw Scott watching her with a strange expression, and then realised what she had done.

'Oh, just a habit I picked up the last few months,' she muttered self-consciously.

Jodi took a deep breath, willing her hands to stay

steady as she picked up a syringe. By the time she had drawn up the local anaesthetic, once again the years of practice at putting aside her personal problems when on duty took over.

Scott had already swabbed the blood away from the wound with normal saline so Jodi could see what she was doing. She looked enquiringly at the pressure pack of anaesthetic spray used to numb the injection sites.

Scott shook his head. 'I think the quicker we get this over the better,' he murmured softly. Louder he said, 'Not scared of a couple of needle pricks, are you, mate? Sister's going to give you a local anaesthetic.'

There was only a faint groan in response, and Jodi took a deep breath and started. Once the anaesthetic had been given time to work, they cleaned the area more thoroughly. Jodi shaved the hair away from the area where the bullet had first sliced open the skin.

'Thank goodness the bullet's not still in there,' she muttered aloud.

Scott grimaced in agreement. 'We wouldn't have been able to risk doing this outside a hospital, in case it was lodged in an artery.'

But I've had to do that! Jodi nearly cried out, but instead bit her bottom lip hard.

'You're shaking!' Scott kept his voice very low, but the alarm still came through. 'Are you sure——?'

'Of course I am,' Jodi managed to snap huskily.

With a tremendous effort, she fought for control again, took a deep breath, and bent over the wound.

'Most of the bleeding is coming from deeper in that hole. Try packing it first,' instructed Scott.

The tourniquet was released a little, but after a brief wait blood started trickling out again.

'No use. Better find where that's coming from,' muttered Scott. He picked up a scalpel, started to hand it to Jodi, and then hesitated. 'Would you like me to have a go at this bit?'

She shook her head, and took it from him. 'It's not my first time,' she assured him through gritted teeth.

Her hand was remarkably steady as she cut open part of the wound along the route of the puncture. Scott managed to help her hold back the layers of muscle and tissue as best he could, and only needed to murmur a couple of instructions as the severed arteries were slowly exposed.

The smallest forceps in the pack were used to clamp off each one, their hands moving in perfect co-ordination, his large ones mopping up so that she could see where to clamp. The emergency pack was very well-equipped with different types of suture thread and clamps. Fortunately, all of the arteries were relatively small, and so she only had to tie them off, not try to repair them.

'It would've been a different story if this had not been caused by a partly spent bullet,' Scott muttered, echoing her own thoughts.

The bullet had only just missed the main anterior tibial artery. As it was, one of the tendons had been slightly damaged.

Scott inspected the tendon carefully. 'I don't think it needs a stitch,' he muttered. 'Just sort out the bleeders.'

'Think you've got them all?' he asked softly a few minutes later.

She nodded. 'We'll soon see.'

'Right, Robert, would you release that tourniquet a bit again, please?' Scott instructed the policeman.

They waited a few moments, and then Jodi thankfully relaxed a little.

'You can take it right off now,' said Scott; 'it's looking fine.'

Jodi spent a few more minutes carefully irrigating the area with saline to try and get rid of any particles of dirt, until Scott said briskly, 'That's enough. Close up now.'

She was starting to realise how very weary she was by the time the absorbable catgut was holding the deeper layers of muscle together, and she started on the last black silk skin sutures.

When Jodi at last stepped back with a deep sigh, Scott said softly, 'One of the best jobs I've seen done.'

'As I said,' Jodi said shakily as she looked at him, 'I've had a lot of practice.'

The memories she'd been holding back with tremendous self-control crowded in suddenly. Horrible memories. Memories that made her suddenly sway.

'Only last week, in fact,' Jodi heard her voice say faintly. Then suddenly the room tilted, and Jodi felt herself starting to fall. She heard Scott's startled exclamation.

'Sorry. . .' she managed, and this time there was no stopping the darkness that descended.

CHAPTER SEVEN

WHEN Jodi opened her eyes, she wondered drowsily why her bed was so narrow, and then realised she was lying on the sofa in the lounge with a blanket over her. She closed her eyes again, and then they flew open as she heard Scott's voice.

'Yes, Robert, I'll make sure she comes to the station in the morning and tells you in detail what happened. But I agree with you. It's pretty clear they were just doing as he said—target practising around what they thought was a vacant house.'

Jodi half sat up, and then fell back as a vicious pain shot through her head. She shuddered. She had actually repaired a bullet wound!

There was the murmur of another voice, and then Scott's again, thanking someone, and saying goodnight.

When he came into the room, Jodi had managed to sit up cautiously and was staring desperately towards the doorway. He paused as he caught sight of her.

'Awake at last.' His face was grim. As he came closer, anger glared at her from his flashing eyes. 'Why on earth didn't you do what I said and lock the back door? I couldn't believe it when I tried the handle and it opened.'

His attack was so unexpected and seemingly out of context that she blinked at him in bewilderment. 'They've gone?' Even to her own ears, her voice sounded far away.

'If you mean that drunken lout, our recent patient, who was enjoying a little rifle practice, yes, or the police, the answer's still yes,' he snapped. 'The police are transporting him to hospital. And you still haven't answered me!'

One hand moved to her throbbing head, and his expression softened a little. Then she stiffened. 'Your hand! I hurt you. . .'

She started to push herself up. He was by her side on the sofa in a moment. 'Take it easy, Jodi. You've been out to it for too long to be going anywhere just yet.'

She sank back, staring helplessly at him. Suddenly he reached down and a little awkwardly gathered her up into his arms.

'Your hand. . .' she began to protest again.

He stared at her as he straightened, his expression altering subtly as he ignored her comment, muttering, 'Bed for you.'

But he didn't move, just sat staring down at her. One of her hands went up to curve around his neck to support herself. His arms tightened convulsively.

'I don't think I've ever been as frightened as I was after you rang me. I was almost here. It was only seconds before I stopped the car, but it seemed like hours.' His voice was very low and tortured.

'And then I hurt you,' Jodi whispered remorsefully. 'You hadn't given me a chance to tell you about the guns, and I was so frightened for you. I tried to see where they were, and then I remembered the door, and——'

It seemed perfectly natural for her hand to slide up into the thick hair at the back of his neck, and to turn her lips to the shelter of his strong neck.

She heard him suck in a breath sharply, and she stilled, realising what she was doing. Then he was striding with her into the bedroom. All the debris from the recent drama was gone, and the sheets and blankets were folded neatly back. Instead of lowering her on to the bed, he sat on the mattress with her still tightly held in his arms.

She started to move away from him, but he was having none of her withdrawal. She looked up at him a little shyly, and then gasped at the blaze of desire on his face. Then his lips were on hers, taking advantage of her open lips to plunder and possess them passionately. For a moment she was passive, and then that inner fire she had felt before when with him flared up, and she was kissing him back as hungrily.

When he at last gave a gasp and buried his face in her hair, she was a quivering, yielding bundle, her arms wrapped around him as tightly as his still were around her.

And she suddenly knew she was feeling gloriously, wonderfully alive as she never had before.

'I knew you were trouble from the moment I saw you,' he muttered harshly.

She stiffened, and dropped her arms. His tightened in response, and then he winced. He muttered something under his breath, and then he had let her go.

She scrambled unsteadily to her feet. 'Your. . .your hand,' she said in a dazed voice, striving desperately for some normality in a world gone crazy.

'It's hurting like blazes,' he said through clenched teeth, in unconscious echo of their patient.

'Oh, Scott,' she wailed, suddenly very close to tears, 'I'm so sorry!'

'And I am too,' he said bleakly as he looked up at

her, cradling his bandaged hand in the other.

She stared blankly back at him as he stood up, towering over her. And she knew it wasn't his hand he was referring to.

As though unable to resist touching her again, he slid the tip of his finger down her cheek. 'I've never lost control like that before, and kissed a woman just after she's recovered from a bad faint.' His lips tilted in self-mockery. 'Hop into bed,' he added gently. 'I won't be far away.'

Her head was still throbbing, and her legs were still like jelly, she acknowledged as she watched him disappear. It's the shock, she tried to convince herself. That's why I responded so. . .so without restraint! Not bothering to change, she crawled into bed, and huddled under the bedclothes, waves of exhaustion sweeping over her.

It wasn't until several hours later that she realised what he had meant by not being far away. The dreams had returned, with all their horror. Then she felt strong arms sheltering her, and as she snuggled into them the dreams disappeared and she slept deeply and peacefully.

She woke as faint light from the rising sun sparkled into the room. In a daze, she thought she must have really dreamed Scott's comforting presence during the night, and then she was suddenly wide awake. A heavy arm was lying across her waist, and a very solid, masculine body was curved against her back. And the arm and the legs were bare! She only hoped that in between had something covering. . .

She tensed as she felt him stir. Then he was still again, and, horrified, she started to edge away from him.

'Mornin', sweetheart,' a sleepy voice drawled softly.

She wrenched herself away from the hand lying dangerously, temptingly, near her breast, and sat up.

'What are you doing in my bed?' she tried to say angrily, but her voice came out in an indignant squeak as her sudden movement revealed a well-muscled, bare chest down to a—she gulped—down to the waistband of a pair of briefs. Muscles rippled enticingly as he put one hand up to rest his head on it. A tremor passed through her from head to toe.

'I'm far too big for that sofa.' He grinned up at her. 'And after your nightmare woke you up it was so comfortable beside you, I yielded to temptation.'

Jodi jumped out of bed, thankful that at least this time she still had her tracksuit on. She stared down at him indignantly.

'Why didn't you make up one of the other beds?' she snapped, feeling heat spreading through her body.

'I love the way red looks on you. Matches the old gold streaks in the hair,' he murmured with a familiar glint in his eyes as he looked her up and down before returning to her face.

She glanced down at her loose, dark green clothes before she realised what he meant. While she glared at him, for a moment speechless, she felt the heat become a furnace in her face.

'As for the other. . .' He waved a bandaged hand at her. 'Didn't want to risk bumping this.'

'Oh!' Remorse struck her again. 'I've already apologised for that,' she muttered.

Scott suddenly flung back the pile of bedding she had dumped on him in her hurry to exit the bed.

'But I'm going to need action, not merely words to prove that,' he said calmly as he stood up.

Jodi hastily averted her eyes as he reached for a pair of trousers neatly folded beside the bed, sat down again and began to step into them awkwardly. Helplessly her eyes swung back as she heard the springs release on the mattress and watched him battle with one hand to pull the trousers up slowly. And up. Over long, very long, firmly muscled, beautifully shaped legs covered by a light sprinkling of dark hair. . . .legs that had fitted so well against hers.

She shivered again, and turned her back hastily on him. She was almost to the door when his last words penetrated.

'Prove what?' she swung back to say, and then gulped as she saw him still trying to tuck in his crumpled shirt with one hand.

'That you're sorry,' he said a little too blandly, not looking at her.

'Of course I'm sorry. I don't go around slamming doors on doctors' fingers on purpose,' she snarled, stifling her instinctive move to go and help him.

'I'm very glad to hear it,' Scot said fervently, and then added, at his most bland again, 'But that still doesn't solve my problem.'

She stared at him, a glimmer of understanding at what he was getting at making her groan inwardly.

'I'm not going to be able to drive very well with this right hand out of action.'

'You'll be a veritable danger on the roads,' flashed back Jodi sarcastically, 'especially with an automatic car!'

'And it'll be extremely hard to do my doctoring properly with my right hand out of action.'

Jodi was silent, staring at him in dismay.

His voice dropped seductively, and to her increasing

alarm he started towards her as he murmured, 'And we made a great team last night, Jodi.'

She opened her mouth, and then closed it again, as he paused in front of her.

'And if you come and help me, I promise there won't be a repeat of last night's huggin' and kissin'.' His eyes suddenly danced with mischief. 'Unless, of course, that promise is going a bit too far.'

'Too far?' Jodi asked in a dazed voice, remembering how wonderful she had felt after that hugging and kissing he referred to so casually.

'I was coming to tell you last night that a relative of mine has agreed to come and chaperon us, if you'll agree to come and stay with me.' His face was suddenly very serious. 'But, after last night, I'm not merely asking. Whether you agree to help me or not, I insist. You're not staying here by yourself!'

She was still staring at him, trying to come to grips with a sudden feeling of tremendous relief, when he suddenly turned and made for the door, saying over his shoulder in what she had come to think of as his normal autocratic tones, 'It won't take long for you to pack while I tidy up for you. It's very early. We'll have breakfast at home so I can take any calls.'

As she walked up the steps at the lovely old house less than an hour later, suddenly it did feel like coming home, certainly far more than her father's house had for a long time.

'You're going crazy,' she muttered angrily to herself as she unpacked her things in the pretty bedroom again. 'You were only here a couple of nights!'

'Jodi! Breakfast's ready,' Scott bellowed from the kitchen.

She felt startled for a moment, and then a faint grin

tilted her lips. Never in a million years would her father have permitted such yelling in his house!

She felt suddenly more light-hearted than she had in a long while as she answered the summons. After all, she could always refuse to have much to do with his patients if she wanted to.

In that, she very quickly was made to realise, she was mistaken.

'After breakfast, I'd promised Beth I'd go and do her physio for her. Now she'll have to be your first patient,' Scott announced calmly when they had almost finished the hearty breakfast of cereal and bacon and eggs. 'Margaret wasn't well herself yesterday when I called back. After that there are some formalities with the police about last night.'

Jodi bit her lip, and sighed inwardly. 'Scott, I don't think I could handle a very heavy work schedule,' she said with a worried frown. 'I'm very much in need of a holiday.'

'I know, Jodi, love.' Scott smiled gently at her. 'I promise I won't overwork you.'

And with that she had to be satisfied.

The beam that spread over Beth's face when Scott explained did wonders in lifting Jodi's spirits and boosting her confidence.

'Great!' Beth enthused. 'You were the best!'

'Oh,' mourned Scott, his good hand on his hip, 'you mean my heroic, energetic thumpin' yesterday was not appreciated?'

'Nope!' grinned Beth cheekily. 'When you first started you were so scared of hurting me, it was like a feather. And when I complained? Too heavy-handed. Nearly cracked one of my ribs at first. Sister Jodi did it like Sister Edith.'

'One up to the nursing profession!' Jodi tossed her head at him, before urging Beth into her room.

As Beth took up her position on the bed over the pillows, she asked in an awed voice, 'Did you really slam the door on Doc's hand?'

Jodi felt a tremor run through her. 'Yes, I'm afraid I did,' she said drily, and added briskly before she had to answer any more questions about an evening—and night—she'd been trying unsuccessfully to forget, 'I'm not sure I can do this as long as the first time.'

'No worry, Sis,' said Beth cheerfully. 'Don't need it quite so long now anyway. Thank goodness!' she added fervently.

After that successful start to the day, things progressed smoothly. Jodi had driven her father's big cars several times over the years. There had been no problems driving them home earlier, and although she had to negotiate a couple of very rough black soil tracks into houses Scott never complained once. In fact, by the time Scott was instructing her where to go for the last call, she was surprised to find she was thoroughly enjoying herself.

'Now, this visit to the Blacks is a little unusual,' Scott said slowly. 'Mrs Black rang me yesterday and invited me to stop off here for a bite of lunch. She rang me up a few times before I went to Sydney insisting Jack was sick, and that he refused to come and have me check him over. She was even more insistent yesterday.'

Jodi glanced across at him with interest, but remained silent, waiting for Scott to give her a brief medical history of his patient as he had before each previous stop.

'You know, I don't think I'll tell you much about

the pair of them, and see if you pick up anything for yourself,' he suddenly said decisively.

'Why? Some kind of test?' Jodi began defensively.

'No, no,' he said quickly, 'They're a pair of absolute old dears. Or they used to be. Jack had a prostratectomy a few weeks back, and it's only been since then that Jill's been claiming he isn't well. And he did actually come for his last check-up a couple of weeks ago. Things were fine then. Now they've even had a few savage arguments about his health, according to her. He still refused to come and see me, and she was worried enough to ring me. Said she didn't want another fight.'

'Do they know I'm coming too?'

Scott didn't answer her.

She glanced across just as he swept a hand through his hair. 'They don't,' she said flatly.

'I'm sorry, I didn't think to ring them. But country people are very hospitable. I'm sure it won't be a problem.'

Jodi wasn't so sure—and even less so when they had stopped the car next to the side-gate in a white picket fence surrounding an old weatherboard farmhouse. When a frail-looking, elderly lady stood up from weeding a flowerbed and peered at them with obvious surprise, she felt even more embarrassed.

'Why, hello—er—er——! Dear me, what a lovely surprise.' Mrs Black smiled at them as she pulled off a pair of very old, mud-caked gardening gloves, and then turned enquiring eyes towards Jodi. 'And your young lady. It's so good of you to call in.'

'Well, you know I can never resist your pumpkin pie, Mrs Black,' Scott said cheerfully as he pushed open the gate for Jodi.

As Jodi looked at Mrs Black, she saw her frown slightly, and look a little puzzled. Then the wrinkled old face looked concerned as Scott added quickly, 'I do apologise for not ringing you to see if you minded Jodi Banner coming for lunch too. She's been helping me this morning.'

Behind them a loud voice from the front veranda of the old weatherboard house said, 'No problem at all, Doc! And hello to you both.'

A look of relief flashed across Mrs Black's face as they turned towards the voice. 'Oh, Jack, dear, you're back from the paddock. Look, these lovely young people have come to see us, and they say——'

'They've come for lunch, love,' the big man moving slowly down the tall flight of steps interrupted them. After he had been introduced to Jodi, he turned to his wife and said very gently, 'Why don't you show them your garden while I finish setting the table and dishing up our lunch?'

The smile that lit his face brought a sudden lump to Jodi's throat. It was so full of love, tenderness and understanding that suddenly she envied them deeply. If they'd had a 'savage argument' recently, there was certainly no tension between them now. They must have both been well into their seventies, but their love was still very real and very strong. For just such a marriage relationship as that had she dreamt for herself over the years.

Their guided tour of the garden took much longer than Jodi had expected. Scott chattered away, showing Jodi a side of him she had not seen before. Soon, as they strolled very slowly around the large yard, he had the little old lady clinging to his arm and laughing gaily at his teasing. He included Jodi in his light-hearted banter, so that Mrs Black called him a rogue very flirtatiously at one stage, and a tinge of red even touched her pale, thin cheeks. He not only charms young ladies and small girls—elderly ladies fall like ninepins too! thought a bemused Jodi.

Lunch consisted of hot soup and bread rolls served on what was obviously the best china in a large, airy dining-room. It was late by the time they were seated, and Jodi felt quite hungry. She was amused that Mrs Black was quite happy to stay seated and leave the serving of their meal to her husband, but bustled around making them their cups of tea.

Jodi watched Mr Black surreptitiously, but he seemed in robust health, and she followed Scott's lead in not referring to their health.

'Sorry there's no pumpkin pie for you today, Doc,' Jack Black said a little abruptly as he cleared their soup bowls away, 'but there's an apple pie with some ice-cream if you like.'

'No, no,' Scott said hurriedly, 'that was more than enough for us. Jodi and I had a late breakfast.'

Mrs Black paused as she set a cup in front of Jodi. 'Breakfast together?' she suddenly snapped loudly. 'What were you doing having breakfast together, may I ask? I do hope——'

'Now, Jill,' interrupted Jack in a soothing voice, 'it's quite OK. The doc had hurt his hand, and Sister Banner had to help him.'

'Oh, you hurt your hand, you poor dear,' cried Mrs Black. 'How ever did you do that?'

Jodi looked at her sharply, and then at Scott. He had already told Jill and Jack about his accident with the door as they had started the meal, when she'd offered to butter his roll. Now he was looking from one elderly face to another. He opened his mouth, but Jack spoke first.

'He had a door slam on his fingers last night, sweetheart. Now what about a cuppa for me, too?'

His wife hesitated, and then trotted obediently back out to the kitchen. When she had disappeared, the old man turned his head and looked at Scott. Jodi's heart ached at the misery and pain in the faded blue eyes. Scott's hand patted the gnarled one on the table next to him.

'Come and see me one day, Jack, and we'll have a chat,' he murmured compassionately.

Jack hesitated, and then nodded briefly as they heard his wife of over fifty years returning.

Jodi and Scott were silent for some time after leaving the Blacks.

It was Jodi who at last broke the silence in a soft voice. 'Alzheimer's?'

'Very possibly.' Scott sighed, and said very quietly, 'She was much worse today than when I saw her when Jack had his operation. I thought she was just upset at him being in hospital. Now I think he's probably been covering up for her for quite some time. Probably the separation and anxiety has made her worse.'

'She hadn't remembered she had invited you for lunch,' Jodi murmured, 'and he handled it so beautifully for her. Not once did he put her down.'

'I don't think she even remembered who I was at first. That's why we took so long outside. It gave him a chance to prepare. Elderly pride is to be cherished and preserved. And people with that rotten memory loss suffer dreadfully from low self-esteem.'

There was silence again.

'It would be wonderful to be loved like that,' Jodi

whispered. 'Especially after all those years.'

'Yes, it would,' murmured Scott huskily. 'It certainly seems to be rarer these days, though. I wonder how they handled all the ups and downs at the beginning of their relationship, as well as down through the years?'

Suddenly he turned towards her, reached over and placed his uninjured hand on her thigh. Heat flooded through Jodi's veins. She glanced at him. His eyes were wistful, and then he smiled so very gently at her. Her eyes returned quickly to the road, her heartbeat accelerating. She hesitated for a moment, and then, as though it had a will of its own, her hand left the steering-wheel and her fingers curled around his.

It seemed so natural. So right. And their hands were still clasped, and resting on her thigh, when they reached home.

CHAPTER EIGHT

THERE was a bright red, latest model sports car parked outside the house as they pulled up.

'Oh, no!' groaned Scott. 'I do believe the cavalry have arrived.'

'The cavalry?'

'What the family seem convinced I need occasionally,' Scott said grimly as he opened his door. 'The last time they thought I needed rescuing they interfered with a very close relationship I had that they considered was detrimental to me.'

Before Jodi could voice the immediate question that flashed into her mind—And were they right?—he had climbed out of the car.

As she grabbed his medical bag from the boot of the car, her mind was in turmoil. Cavalry? Why on earth would his family think he needed rescuing now? The obvious answer was just too, too ludicrous.

Scott was waiting for her to catch up with him at the foot of the steps as she activated the central-locking device. Instead of insisting that he could manage the bag as he had done at every visit, he clutched at her free hand. She tried to tug it away, but he held it firmly as they started up the steps.

'Well,' drawled a husky female voice, 'it's about time!'

Scott scowled at the woman sprawled elegantly on a cane chair on the veranda. 'When did you get here?'

Jodi watched curiously as a lithe body clad in a very

tight cream sweater and red miniskirt pushed herself slowly erect. She dropped the end of the cigarette in her hand and crunched it out with one very high-heeled scarlet sandal. Her dainty legs were encased in sheer red nylon.

'There's an ashtray on that table next to you, if you must smoke,' Scott snapped disapprovingly. 'And what are you doing here?'

Large blue eyes widened further. 'Your mother rang mine and said you needed help.'

'My mother!' Scott groaned. 'I rang Aunt Merle to see if she could come and stay for a week or so!'

'And apparently she found out she couldn't after all. Jean went into hospital early. She tried to ring you back, and when she couldn't get you rang your mother, who rang mine. And here I am!' She beamed at him, and then looked pointedly at Jodi. Her smile slipped as it took in their clasped hands.

Jodi pulled her hand frantically away, feeling the blush stealing into her cheeks, despite holding the younger woman's now openly hostile gaze.

'Behave yourself, Lizzy!' Scott said with a steely note in his voice. 'This is Jodi Banner, who's had a bad time recently. Jodi, this is my cousin, Liz Campbell.'

'Elizabeth, thank you, Scott,' frowned his cousin, all but ignoring Jodi. 'I haven't been called Liz for years. And I'm a very distant cousin.'

'I've never called you anything else! And you are my first cousin,' Scott said through clenched teeth.

Red lips pouted. 'But that's only *your* pet name, Scott, darling. You shouldn't introduce me like that.'

Jodi saw the storm clouds darkening on Scott's face, and hastened to say firmly, 'I'm glad you were able to come, Elizabeth. And now I'm afraid we've had a very busy day so far, which isn't over yet by any means, and——'

'And now I'm here to help!' Liz said triumphantly.

'With the housekeeping. Only!' Scott snapped emphatically. 'Now, if I could have my keys, please, Jodi——'

'You let her drive you?' gasped Liz, 'In that car?'

Scott raised his eyebrows at her as he took the keys from Jodi, and then proceeded to unlock the door. She tensed, waiting for him to tell his cousin what had happened to his hand.

'I'm quite sure Aunt told Mum, and Mum told you all about my hurting my hand, Lizzy,' Scott said sarcastically. 'So stop the dramatics. Right now!' he added, and glared at her for a moment before nodding to Jodi to go into the house.

'The car has to be re-stocked for the next round,' he said to Jodi as he started for the surgery. 'You come too, and I'll show you where everything is. We'll see you after you settle in, Liz,' he tossed over his shoulder as his cousin tapped her way behind them.

'Scott!' wailed Liz, 'I did come to help you!'

Jodi glanced back at the girl, and paused. She was really very young, and looked genuinely disappointed. Frowning slightly, Jodi said loudly to Scott's still retreating back, 'I'd really prefer to rest for a while, Scott. Why don't you sort things out with Li—er—Elizabeth, and I'll meet you back in the surgery later?'

'No!' Scott snapped, and turned to face her. 'I could get called out again, and there are several things I don't like not having ready. We'll do it now.'

He did not even bother to look at the now forlorn-looking young woman before turning on his heel again. Suddenly Jodi felt sorry for her, and angry at him.

'*You'll* do it now! I'll help Elizabeth bring in her things. After all, she has come to help.' Jodi didn't wait to see his reaction as she walked towards Liz. 'Have you got much to bring in out of your lovely car? I can help, if you like.'

Jodi nearly laughed out loud at the astonishment that first spread across the young face, followed rapidly by awe. They were both silent as Scott's footsteps paused briefly and then continued stomping down the corridor. They both jumped as the door of the surgery slammed shut.

Suddenly a friendly grin spread over Liz's face. 'Wow! He didn't even tear a strip off you!'

'Not that time,' Jodi said grimly, and added rapidly as she saw the question forming in Liz's eyes, 'We'd better hurry, though, and get you settled. I should be assisting him.'

By the time Jodi had helped to bring in a pile of books, several items thrown haphazardly into the car as well as a very large suitcase, and collected linen and blankets, all Scott's cousin's initial reserve and suspicion had disappeared. Liz began to chat away as though she had known Jodi forever. It turned out she was in her final year at the University of Southern Queensland in Toowoomba studying nursing.

To Jodi's query about whether she was enjoying it or not, she was suddenly very serious. 'Yes, I do enjoy the course, but I'm not sure I'm going to be a very good practical nurse. We still have more time to spend in clinical work yet, but I'm finding out that sick people scare the life out of me.'

'Yes, there are still times when they do that to me, too,' Jodi said grimly. 'But there are plenty of different fields that your nursing training will open up for you.'

'Do you like being a nurse, Jodi?'

Jodi stilled. Once she would not have hesitated in giving an unqualified 'yes'. There had been times this last year when she had thought she hated it. But today. . .

She thought of Beth's beaming smile. Then there had been the relief in another elderly patient as she'd finished changing the dressing on her badly ulcerated leg. Certainly it had been an odorous, unpleasant task, but now she remembered the thrill of pleasure and satisfaction she had felt when she was whole-heartedly thanked for such a relatively simple thing, and assured that it felt 'so much better now, love'.

'I think I've worked in high-pressured areas for too long a spell where not many of my patients recovered,' she said very softly at long last, acknowledging the truth for the first time. Jodi looked across the bed at Liz, who was watching her curiously. 'They. . .they weren't able to tell me if my nursing made much difference to them. I. . .I think we always need to be able to distance ourselves to a certain extent from the suffering we see. Being objective, I think your tutors probably call it. I've never found that easy, and lately I found that harder and harder to do, and then. . .'

She hesitated again. Suddenly she realised that deep inside her she had become so swamped by people's suffering that she'd gone to the other extreme. To survive she had tried to cut her emotions off from them. That had been impossible to do completely, but undoubtedly it had made her a much poorer nurse. She had been very irritable with staff and patients alike, and instead of easing her stress had only made the whole situation more tense and more stressful.

I honestly thought before today that I couldn't bear

to be a nurse any more, was on the tip of her tongue, but something in the eager young face waiting for her answer stopped her.

'I guess most nurses find there are times when they love it and times when they hate it,' she said gently instead.

'Jodi!' Scott's voice sounded exasperated as it roared through the house.

Jodi straightened, and pulled a face. 'Does he always yell inside like that?'

Liz giggled. 'Usually. Especially when he's mad. And it's me he's mad at.' She hesitated, her face becoming serious. 'He. . .he cares too much sometimes. He was pretty badly hurt last year, Jodi. There was a woman. . .' She stopped abruptly, and then added quickly, 'Well, his mother was very worried about him. We all were. He has been back to his old self recently, and when he rang my aunt and she couldn't come. . .well, it was so unlike him to admit he needed help that they. . .we. . .'

'The family sent in the cavalry,' Jodi said very quietly as Liz's voice faded away in some confusion. 'But I can assure you the cavalry isn't necessary because of me.'

Liz looked startled. 'Cavalry?' A slow smile spread across her face again. 'Is that what Scott said?'

Jodi nodded. 'When he saw your car.'

Liz glanced down at her very sexy outfit, and her face was full of mischief when she looked back at Jodi. Jodi felt her lips twitch at her expression and suddenly both women were laughing.

'A man less likely to need someone coming to his rescue I've yet to meet,' gasped Jodi at last.

Liz sobered quickly. 'Perhaps.' She searched Jodi's face. 'He's one of the finest men I've ever known.

Also the only big brother I've ever had,' she added swiftly as Jodi lost every desire to smile. 'But sometimes a man's very integrity and loyalty can. . .can trap him.'

Jodi's eyes widened. Scott trapped? What on earth——?

'Jodi! Get your butt in here!' The roar was even louder.

'Oops! He's getting madder,' drawled Liz. 'You'd better go.'

'No way,' Jodi said calmly. 'I'll finish helping you first, Elizabeth.'

Liz laughed again and looked at her with sudden respect. 'Good. You'll do, and please call me Liz. He gets my back up too.'

'That why you provoke him?'

Mischief filled the laughing eyes. 'You bet!'

Then as Liz looked at Jodi a very thoughtful expression chased away the laughter. 'Last year, I turned up at his house in Sydney without any warning too.' She pulled a face. 'In even more provocative gear, I'm afraid.'

Liz paused, and then she scowled. 'His long-time girlfriend had just become his very new fiancée, to the horror of the family, I might add. She was a very hoity-toity madam, and he'd somehow let her push him into becoming a surgeon, when he'd always wanted to be a GP. Anyway, she objected strongly to my living with him. Scott saw a different side to her entirely when she wouldn't believe we were relatives. Come to think of it, I don't think he tried very hard to convince her. . .'

Poor Scott, thought Jodi. But then she wondered if the family had been right about him letting anyone push him into anything he didn't want to do. He was too forceful a personality. Unless he had loved his ex-fiancée very much. . .

Jodi watched Liz musing for a moment, and then asked softly, 'You were the cavalry?'

Liz chuckled. 'Well, they did have a rather horrific row about me,' she drawled, her eyes sparkling with triumph, 'and they split up, much to everyone's relief.'

'So the cavalry did arrive in the nick of time,' Jodi murmured, and they grinned at each other.

Jodi was still smiling when she walked into the surgery several minutes later.

'Glad to see you're so happy taking your time, Sister Banner,' Scott snarled at her. 'Now, if you wouldn't mind——'

'Oh, but I do, Dr Campbell,' she interrupted sweetly.

He looked blankly at her.

'I do mind,' she said patiently, as though speaking to a child, 'being bossed around, being roared at!'

He continued to stare at her for a moment, and then his own lips suddenly twitched. 'I boss you around?'

'Yes.'

'I roar at you?'

She nodded, and than snapped out, 'You certainly do!'

There was silence as they stared at each other, neither giving ground. Then a familiar flame flared to life in his eyes. She trembled.

He took a step closer. 'Have you ever stopped to wonder why?'

'Why?' she croaked.

'Why I boss you around, why I yell. . .'

She refused to step back as he came closer still.

'Because while I'm doing that to you it's easier to keep my hands off you!' he said in a driven voice.

Her nerve broke, and she whirled away from him as his hands went out to touch her.

'Well, I suggest you think of another cure, Doctor, or you won't have a nurse, or housekeeper!'

'Oh, for goodness' sake!' he roared.

Jodi put her hands over her ears, glared at him and turned on her heel.

She was at the door before he said quickly, in a very controlled voice, 'Jodi, I really need you to help me here. OK, OK! I apologise for being bossy and yelling, but for goodness' sake give me a hand here, will you?'

She turned back reluctantly. He pointed to a large bottle in an open cupboard.

'I don't think I'd better try and pick up that chlorhexidine solution with one hand, and I need it to soak the thermometers in I've used. Also, there's a large box out in the car that we need.'

Silently she approached him. He moved out of her way, and as he did so her heart melted as she suddenly realised how tired and worn he looked.

'They rarely use these old glass ones in the large modern hospitals now,' she muttered, more for something to break the tension than anything.

'I know,' he said impatiently.

She bit her lip, and without any further protest she followed his precise instructions in preparation for the next day.

'Well, I've only to put a couple of things in my black bag, and that should do it,' Scott said wearily after they had finished packing disposable sterile dressing-trays and various-sized syringes, a selection of separately packaged dressings, lotions and bandages into the large box she had collected from the car.

'But we didn't use many of these today at all,' Jodi said, feeling slightly puzzled.

'I know,' he said in a suddenly cross voice. 'I didn't need anything out of the box until today, and discovered it hadn't been refilled. One of the doctors from the practice in Toowoomba has been doing my rounds, and was to catch a plane to go on holidays. The arrangement was for him to drive his car to Brisbane so I'd have it to get home with. He didn't re-stock. Probably ran out of time. I should have checked before, but I only discovered it yesterday. There was no time this morning,' he added gruffly.

'*His* car?'

Scott raised his head and looked blankly at her.

'That. . .that Mercedes I've been driving isn't even yours?' Her voice rose.

'Do you think anyone in their right mind would drive a car like that all the time over those rough roads the way we have today?' he snapped irritably. 'I didn't even bring mine here from Sydney. Been using Edith's Land Rover. It's getting some repairs done on it. I'm supposed to pick it up some time, but there just hasn't been much spare time.'

She thought of the day before. There had been very little time that day too, partly because of her, she thought guiltily.

'Why. . .why did you let me think it was yours?'

He looked at her a little warily. 'Would you believe to boost myself up in your eyes? Well, at first, that is, before I found out what you thought,' he added hurriedly.

She studied him for a moment, thinking of his natural friendliness with his patients, from the poorest home to the richest. And then why hadn't he told her when she had slammed the door?

'No,' she said baldly, 'I wouldn't believe you.'

His expression softened slightly as he stared at her, and then he turned away as he said quickly, 'We'll try and pick up the Land Rover tomorrow.'

She watched his broad back thoughtfully. A twinge of hurt sliced through her that he had not minded what she had thought of him. Then she stiffened at another thought. Or had he not told her because he had wanted to watch her reaction to find out more about her?

Scott said over his shoulder, 'Perhaps we'd better make time before surgery to re-dress my hand.'

'Oh, yes, of course,' she mumbled, suddenly ashamed that she had not offered before this. 'Is your hand still painful, Scott?' she asked quietly.

He looked up at her, and then shrugged.

'Do you think it needs an X-ray?' she asked with a frown.

'It's only across the three fingers. Fortunately,' he said lightly.

'All the same, I'd better do it straight away. I should have done that this morning first thing.'

He hesitated, and she cursed her stupid tongue. There was no way she wanted to remind him of their encounter that morning. Carefully she avoided his eyes as he reluctantly sat down while she collected what she needed.

Jodi bit her lip when she saw the bruised and swollen fingers. But she was even more dismayed by the angry-looking area around the cuts.

'This is pretty badly infected, Scott,' she said as calmly as she could. 'Do you have any anti-biotics here?'

'Oh, for crying out loud, it only needs some disinfectant,' he said hurriedly.

'I really think it needs more than that,' Jodi said dubiously.

'Of course it doesn't,' Scott snapped impatiently.

Very reluctantly, Jodi had to be satisfied with swabbing the cuts with betadine. 'What about leaving the dressing off for a while so it can dry out?' she urged.

'No way,' he snorted. 'It's only a couple of hours to afternoon surgery. I don't want everyone gawking at it. Just put the dressing and bandage back on, that's a good girl, and then we might both be able to have a rest before we have to start again.'

Jodi was relieved to be able to lie down for a while. As she relaxed, though, she was still concerned about Scott's hand. Doctors and nurses were notoriously bad patients, and she wished she had been more persistent about the antibiotics.

Then, as she lay staring at the window, she dwelt on her conversation with Liz. Scott was no wimp. Perhaps he had been glad deep down of an excuse to have the engagement stopped. The woman Jodi had mentioned must have been why Scott had told her at the airport that he was 'off' all women. And he certainly would be fed up with Liz. No doubt he still resented the family's interference, too.

But it must be rather wonderful to have a family who went to bat for you because they loved you so much, Jodi thought wistfully.

Even when her mother had been alive, she had so rarely been able to be involved in her children's lives. Her father never had until they were approaching university years. Her lips curled. Even then it had been because of his own selfish reasons, his own prestige in the high-society crowd he mixed with.

Jodi rolled over on to her back, switching her thoughts deliberately from the hurts of the past to her immediate future. What was she going to do about supporting herself? The thought of returning to nursing made her shiver.

Then she remembered her own words to Liz. There were other options than hospital-based nursing care. Community nursing? Industrial? Working for private pathologists? Doctors' surgeries? Rural nursing?

A slight smile twitched her lips. If today was any indication at all, district nursing might not be too bad. Certainly it would be a far less pressured type of work. Or had it been so enjoyable just because of the company?

She stirred restlessly. Scott's patients thought the world of him. When he had let Beth tease him, he had been incredibly attractive. She thought with regret of their arrival home. For such a brief time they had shared a closeness she had never experienced before. So many firsts with him, she suddenly realised grimly.

And now she had to admit that her first feeling at seeing they had a visitor had been disappointment that the promise of his hand on her thigh would not be fulfilled with. . .with. . .

You stupid idiot, she castigated herself silently. He was only being comforting. Friendly.

But did 'friendliness' make her tingle as she had all over when she'd touched him, even accidentally? He'd had a bad effect on her nervous system even when she had been attending to his hand. And those kisses earlier had most certainly not been just friendly ones!

She groaned. No mere friend could set the blood boiling and pulsing through her body the way he did when he kissed and caressed until she was on fire to be even closer to him. On fire as she was now, even thinking about those kisses! And he expected her to stay and help him indefinitely?

She groaned. 'You'd better only be on a three-week holiday, Jimmy, dear. I think I might be in big trouble!'

CHAPTER NINE

Two weeks later, Jodi did not just suspect she was in deep trouble. She was certain of it.

When she had walked reluctantly into the surgery the evening Liz had arrived, Scott had glanced sharply at her pale face, and said quietly, 'Liz has offered to help me here. Why don't you see where she's up to in preparing our tea, and take over there?'

Jodi had hesitated, and then given a brief, relieved nod before going to find Liz.

Liz had been ecstatic. 'Really?' she had beamed. 'He wasn't at all keen on me helping him tonight.'

'Well, I'm afraid I haven't been well, and I'm supposed to be on holidays,' Jodi had told her, adding hopefully, 'Perhaps he'll let you drive him tomorrow as well.'

But Scott had grunted a definite, 'No way!' to that suggestion, pointing out that there could be things she would have to do for him that legally Liz could not yet do. At the house, he could call Jodi if he needed her.

Jodi's heart had sunk as Liz had pulled a disappointed face, admitting that she did have lectures she should not really miss.

The days that followed had fallen into a pattern. Liz looked after the house as best she could between study commitments, and helping occasionally with the surgery. In reality they had ended up seeing very little of her.

Jodi had discovered that Scott's surgery was actually

the rural side of a much larger practice. The appointments for them were made through the secretaries at the main surgery on the outer suburb in Toowoomba, and phoned through to Scott. At least once during that first week, a bright young woman secretary from there had appeared to get some bookwork to do from Scott's office. One morning a week, Liz's lectures and tutorials had coincided with Scott's relief work at the city surgery, and he had gone off with her in the fiesty little sports car, to Liz's great delight.

The variety of patients' complaints on the home visits had rather surprised Jodi at first. But then she had reminded herself that quite a few of their calls was to give treatment that was really a district nurse's task.

Their routine included giving daily insulin injections to a couple of elderly diabetics who could not be trusted to draw up their own correct dosages. There had been chronic ulcers to dress, even that of a thin, angular man who still had a wound that had needed dressing since a World War II injury. He was remarkably philosophical about it, daring her from sharp eyes under his thick white bushy eyebrows to pity him.

There had been regular visits this past week to one old gentleman in the terminal stages of lung cancer. He apparently alternated between his two daughters. One lived in the city, but he always preferred his visit out to the country. He was never far from a cylinder of oxygen, and several times they had been called to give pain-relief injections.

Jodi had found herself tensing on their first visit, once again feeling the sense of hopelessness and helplessness that terminally ill patients had increasingly made her feel. But it had been a surprisingly cheerful time.

The old man had been able to wheeze out a few jokes that had made Scott put back his head and give a bellow of laughter. Then on another occasion the grey-faced old man had very slyly succeeded in making her blush by his innuendoes to Scott about his beautiful young nurse.

'Reckon I wouldn't mind havin' a busted hand either if it keeps a beauty like 'er at me beck an' call,' he had smirked.

At the time, Jodi had been surprised when Scott had turned quickly away, ignoring the comment, when usually he would have come back with a crack of his own.

By the end of the first week, Jodi had been pleasantly surprised how much she was enjoying herself. After the first few days' rush of catching up, the rounds had been mostly relaxed, with time for a chat or even accepting the inevitably proffered refreshments.

And now, although Scott's hand had healed enough for him not to need her to help him with the 'doctorin',' as he called it, he still insisted it became too painful if he had to drive the Land Rover over the rough roads.

'I suppose a change is as good as a holiday,' she mused out loud suddenly as they left their last patient early on another clear, sunny Friday afternoon.

Scott gave a low laugh. 'I felt that my first couple of weeks here. I was even twice as busy then as we are now.' He settled back more comfortably in his seat, resting his head back with a sigh. 'Sure beats the mad rush of a surgical registrar's life in a hospital.'

'And the life in an intensive care unit,' smiled Jodi.

'You said you worked there for five years? You must have enjoyed it.'

Jodi thought about that for a moment. 'Yes, I

certainly did to start with,' she said slowly. 'There was a great deal of excitement. Something always happening. Life and death issues far more than in the wards. I enjoyed having my knowledge and abilities stretched to their limits. In the end, though, I think I'd begun to dread each shift.'

'Why did you stay so long, then?' Scott asked casually.

Jodi shrugged. 'I'm not really sure now. Probably several reasons really. Other jobs weren't easy to come by. Other jobs seemed boring in comparison.'

She fell silent. And my father would have thought any other work even more beneath me, she could have added.

After a moment she gave a bitter little laugh, and said without thinking, 'Just over two weeks ago I'd have given anything to be back in a so-called boring job. Any other job would have done, even sweeping out toilets!'

'And two weeks ago you were in Africa?'

Scott was still lying back with his eyes closed when she glanced swiftly at him. But suddenly she knew he was listening very intently.

'Yes, in Africa!' she said abruptly, and before he could ask any more she changed the subject swiftly, 'How much longer are you going to be working here, Scott?'

Scott stirred. He sighed and sat up, turning to look at her. She kept her eyes determinedly fixed on the road ahead.

'Why did you decide to go to Africa, Jodi?'

Jodi swallowed rapidly. What the real answer to that was she still wasn't quite sure. She had been out of work for a while and had to give up her flat near the hospital, and she had moved back home with her father at his insistence—a bad mistake!

The work in the mission hospital she had heard of at her church one Sunday when she had been feeling very down had definitely appeared to be challenging and different. Perhaps unconsciously, she had wanted to go as far away as possible from people who knew her well. The pressure from her father had perhaps only been the last straw.

'What happened in Africa, Jodi?'

The car swerved slightly. 'Nothing I want to talk about,' she said a little too loudly as she tightened her grip on the wheel.

The first couple of days, Jodi had been waiting for Scott to probe into her past. It had surprised her at first that he had not insisted they have the 'talk' he had promised her. But then she had relaxed, even feeling a little resentful that he had apparently lost interest in her.

Not once had he even tried to touch her, let alone kiss her again! At first she had put that down to the arrival of the 'cavalry', as he had called Liz, but then she'd had to accept that she just wasn't the type to attract a handsome doctor like him, refusing to acknowledge that she missed those particular attentions.

'Have you talked about it to anyone?' the relentless soft tones insisted.

She had been lost in her thoughts and memories, and started as he spoke.

'Talked? Talked about—oh!'

'No, you couldn't have,' Scott murmured thoughtfully. 'You said you'd only just arrived back when we met, didn't you?'

'Heavens! That seems so long ago,' Jodi said brightly. 'And I'm glad both Bill and Vera Wood are doing so well.'

Scott snorted at her feeble attempt to change the subject. 'Whatever happened isn't going to go away because you refuse to talk about it, Jodi. It's more likely simply to burrow in deeper and fester.'

'Why the sudden interest again, Scott?' she said as calmly as she could.

'Believe me, the interest has always been there, Jodi,' His voice was sharp. 'I stopped asking before because you became so upset at the thought of it all. And you couldn't have coped with any more pressure, especially after that shooting episode! And why now?' He turned his head and she felt his eyes sweeping over her. When he spoke again, his voice was husky. 'Because your brother should be home any day now, and because at last you've lost those hollow eyes with dark rings around them. A bit pale still by the end of the day, but you are eating and sleeping better now, aren't you?'

There were still some days when she felt unnaturally very weary, but Jodi's mirror had been telling her that she was looking much better. She glanced at him with a slight smile.

'Still red-haired and anorexic-looking, though?'

'Never call that gorgeous head of shining auburn merely red!' he protested.

Jodi felt the heat mounting in her cheeks. 'You did!' she snapped.

'Me? Never!'

Jodi heard the smile in his voice, and swallowed. By now she knew without daring to look at him how that smile would have started in dark, twinkling eyes, spreading slowly across his face, the dimple perhaps peeping out briefly, a gleam of even white teeth. She had found herself, the past few days particularly, looking out for it. It was just one of the many, many things she loved about him.

The car swerved again.

'Jodi!' protested Scott. Then he added firmly, 'I'm sorry, I shouldn't have started this while you were driving. We'll discuss it later.'

Discuss it later? thought Jodi a little hysterically. Discuss what later? Her red hair? Africa? Certainly not discuss her falling in love with him!

How could she have been such a fool? She had let herself love him, and she was in deep, deep trouble!

Helplessly she acknowledged that it had probably been inevitable from their first stunning kiss. A fact she had refused to admit until now, but the real reason why she had insisted on moving to her brother's.

Jodi shook her head, trying to clear her suddenly blurred eyes. Fortunately they were almost home, and she automatically slowed down to make the turn into their driveway, her body tense.

'Madam Liz isn't home yet. I thought she'd be back in time for afternoon tea today,' Scott commented.

Jodi blinked, forcing her mind to focus on what he had just said. 'No,' she managed to say as normally as she could, 'didn't she tell you she had a date?'

Scott straightened. 'No, she did not, the young monkey!'

Jodi glanced at him with surprise. 'Should she have?'

'You'll have to do surgery, and I know you hate it,' he said angrily.

Jodi drew in a sharp breath as she stopped the car. She stared blindly through the windscreen and muttered, 'I didn't know you knew that.'

He snorted. 'How could I help but notice when you freeze up every time with the patients, and are so irritable before and afterwards?'

Jodi bit her lip. 'I'm. . .I'm sorry Scott. I've tried hard, but I. . . I. . .' Her voice faded away, and she groped for the door-handle.

How could she tell him that it was the fact it reminded her too much of Africa? It was stupid, she knew. Here there were fresh flowers in the waiting-room, comfortable chairs, magazines to read, no emaciated bodies from starvation.

But sometimes it was so horribly similar to the clinics in Africa. The patients would watch her expectantly as she entered the room. And it was their eyes that haunted her. . .always the eyes. Anxious eyes. . . resigned eyes. . .hopeless eyes. . .

She was very quiet as they unloaded the car. Scott was silent too as he helped her. It wasn't until they had finished tidying up, and replenishing stock, that he said very quietly, 'Jodi, these past couple of weeks you've been a tremendous help, but you are still standing back from our patients. Some of them even think you're stuck-up.'

She turned on him furiously.

He held up a hand, and continued sharply, 'Except with Beth and Margaret Field, and why they are the exception I haven't worked out yet, but to almost everyone else you give the impression of not wanting to encourage any conversation with them except what is needed professionally.'

She stared back at him helplessly.

'And that's one reason why I still think you should try and talk about what has happened to you.'

His face was stern, but his eyes were compassionate. She couldn't hold his gaze, and walked away to the window.

'How many times do I have to tell you I *can't* talk about it?' Jodi cried desperately. 'I. . .I'm scared of going to pieces. . . I——'

'Perhaps you need to let go. And I'd be here to pick up the pieces, sweetheart.' His voice was low and filled with tenderness.

Jodi felt him just behind her. She swung around, her mouth quivering helplessly. He reached for her, but she fended him off.

'You. . .you'll hate me like everyone else when. . . when you know. . .' she managed bitterly. It was even harder to tell him now than before, when she had only wanted his good opinion. Now she craved for him to love her.

She swallowed painfully, forcing herself to continue. 'I've thought quite a bit about what you said about burnout. I. . .I think now you may be right. It wasn't just what happened a couple of weeks ago. I. . .I was forced to resign from IC over six months ago.' Jodi felt the scorching shame sweep through her as it had so many, many times before. 'I. . .I made a very bad mistake, and. . .and——'

They both started as someone rang a long peal on the front doorbell.

Scott muttered something under his breath. His hand reached up and touched her cheek very gently. Electricity shot through her.

'I don't think I could ever hate you, Jodi Banner,' he murmured. He stood there for a moment, looking deeply into her eyes.

She drew in a sharp breath at what she thought she

saw in his face. There was another long, impatient peal on the doorbell.

Scott turned and started towards the doorway. Then he paused, and said emphatically, 'This conversation is only postponed this time. And in the meantime use your nursing skills to think about it. You'll have to admit that you do need to talk out what is traumatising you. If not to me, than I'll set up an appointment with a professional counsellor.'

Jodi gasped in protest, but he had disappeared, his firm steps sounding on the wooden floorboards of the veranda as he left the surgery by the side-door.

Professional counselling!

She moved on trembling legs and sank on to a chair. These past days she had begun to feel so much better that she had been only too willing to push out of her mind what had brought her fleeing to find her brother, even a brother she had seen very little of during the past ten years.

As she had admitted in the car, she was definitely feeling quite a bit better physically. But there were still too many nights sleep disturbed by dreams. Dreams of violence and death that had her waking up shaking, and covered in sweat from head to toe.

It was as though she had been almost in limbo during the daylight hours, since she had returned to this house from that night of fear and anguish. Now she realised how she had really only been drifting with the tide of events each day had brought. She had rarely been by herself, except when she had been so tired she had fallen into bed.

She had even welcomed having to drive Scott around, perhaps even welcomed having to help him with patients. It had filled her mind with other thoughts, and it had all seemed so different in the patients' own homes. So less threatening. It had prevented her from thinking, remembering.

But still, deep down, she had been frightened. Frightened that her fragile inner being couldn't risk letting the patients really matter to her again. And only Beth had crept past that barrier.

And she had been thinking all along that Scott had not known.

He was a very good, observant doctor, she thought bitterly, too good sometimes!

She raised her head sharply as she heard men's voices approaching. Her eyes were burning, and she wished desperately that she had taken the opportunity to make herself scarce, especially if Scott had a patient to see.

By the time she had darted to her feet and was on her way to the door, it was too late. Scott pushed open the door violently, and stood there glaring at her.

'I've known all along your brother didn't know you were coming here, but why on earth didn't you at least tell your father where you were?' he accused her furiously.

And then another man, also strong-jawed and imposing, had elbowed his way past Scott. He also was furiously angry as he glared in utter amazement at Jodi. But this man's dark hair was heavily streaked with grey. This man she had known, and been in awe of, all her life.

'Father!' she gasped faintly, staring at him with dawning horror. 'What on earth are you doing here?'

CHAPTER TEN

'JODI? It *is* you!'

Her father reached her in a couple of strides. His arms grasped her so tightly above both her elbows that she gave a little gasp of pain.

He released his grip a little, but then his hands moved to her shoulders and he gave her a little shake, biting out harshly, 'Where have you been? I've never been so bewildered. . .so. . .so worried.'

'Where have I been?' She gazed into his eyes with disbelief. 'But you knew I went to Africa!'

'But I didn't know you'd come home so early!' His voice rose and his eyes flashed ferociously. His hands tightened cruelly again, and this time he shook her harder.

Her teeth met as her head jerked. She winced, and tried to pull herself free, suddenly feeling frightened that he might hit her as he had in her teens. A large hand came over and clamped down on one of her father's wrists.

'I don't think shaking her is going to achieve anything,' Scott snarled angrily.

Jodi looked at him with dazed eyes. He looked as furious as her father. She wasn't sure if it was with her or the older man.

'Well, something needs to be done to her to bring her to her senses,' David Banner senior snarled back, but his hands did fall away from her, and Jodi took a quick step away from him. Her face had lost all its colour as she looked from one man to the other.

Then Scott moved, and she felt his strong arm come around her shoulders. She was trembling, and let her body lean into his strength.

She had been so right to compare Scott with her father when she had first seen him sitting across from her in that plane. Both were big men, with handsome good looks. Both were men whose very personalities could dominate those around them. Both could be very intimidating.

But suddenly the comparison stopped right there. She knew Scott would never, ever hurt her, always protect her, even as he was now. Love for him washed through her, easing a little of the hurt caused by her own father.

David Banner turned on Scott, staring at him suspiciously. 'Who the hell are you, telling me how to treat my own daughter?' he snapped furiously.

'I told you my name was Scott Campbell, *Dr* Scott Campbell.' Scott's voice was like chips of ice. 'And I happen to be Jodi's doctor, and I'm telling you Jodi has been under too much strain to be subjected to more like this.'

Then Scott let her go, actually turning his back on the older man as he faced her. Jodi stared at him in a daze. He was her doctor?

'Your father called in here to ask for directions to your brother's place when he saw the surgery sign out the front. Ann asked him to go to their house to pick up some things——'

'*Ann* asked. . .!'

Her father reached out as though to grab at her arm again. She snatched it away before he touched her, but then froze as he roared, 'Your brother's lying in a coma, and you disappear off the face of the earth, you selfish——'

'Be quiet!' roared Scott even louder.

In one movement he had pushed—pushed!—her father out of the way and had an arm around Jodi's waist, guiding her now shaking body to the nearest chair. For a moment Jodi wasn't sure which shocked her the most—the horror of what her father had said, or the fact that someone had dared to stand up to him like that!

'Don't you dare push me around, you young. . .' Dr David Banner was actually spluttering with outrage.

'Jimmy. . .' Jodi couldn't take her eyes from Scott's as he crouched beside her.

'He just told me that they were involved in a bus accident on the way back from North Queensland, and are recovering in hospital in Brisbane,' Scott said swiftly, completely ignoring the older man, his eyes filled now with concern, his hands holding both of hers comfortingly. 'That's all I know yet, I brought him straight to you, but now. . .'

Jodi helplessly stared past him towards her father. For the first time ever, her father looked his age. He was pale and drawn, deep lines etched in his face.

'How bad. . .?' she managed through dry lips.

Scott looked up at her father also. 'Is your son still unconscious?'

'No,' the older man snapped. He hesitated, and then said quickly, 'He was for about twenty-four hours. No cerebral haemorrhage, just concussion and a back injury. Not talking much yet.'

Jodi suddenly realised she was clinging to Scott's hands as though to a lifebelt. Her imploring eyes turned to him.

'And his wife and daughter?' Scott asked for her abruptly.

'My. . .my granddaughter. . .' The harsh tones faltered for a moment. 'My granddaughter miraculously escaped with some minor cuts and bruising. Ann has broken her arm and leg, a fractured femur and a Colles's fracture.'

Jodi shut her eyes tightly. They were alive. They were all alive.

'But what on earth are you doing here, Jodi?' her father demanded in a tightly controlled voice.

Once again Scott answered for her. 'She came here to see her brother.'

'Why on earth didn't you come home? Why on earth didn't you let me know where you were?' Her father's voice started to rise again. 'I didn't even know you had left Africa until that missionary bloke rang to see how you were a week ago. He was most upset that I hadn't heard from you. And so was I, young lady, so was I! People have been asking me all kinds of awkward questions since a local TV news report. What was I supposed to say to them without being made to look a downright fool? It's not normal for a man not to know where his own daughter's gone after she's been through such a dreadful experience!'

Jodi pulled her hands away from Scott and brushed away the couple of tears that had escaped down her cheeks. 'I. . .you and I'd had such a row. . .and,' she choked out, 'I couldn't take any more. . .'

Scott stood up. 'There's no need to talk about any of that now,' he said decisively, 'You want to go to Brisbane?' he shot at Jodi. When she nodded fervently, he turned back to Dr Banner. 'I suggest you go and pick up what your daughter-in-law wants and go on back to Brisbane. I'll make sure Jodi gets to the hospital. Which one are they in?'

Jodi watched her father open and close his mouth as he actually gaped at the stern young man confronting him. Then, to her utter amazement, he told them which hospital before turning towards Jodi. She saw his face harden again, but before he could speak Scott was holding her by the arm and propelling her from the chair and towards the door, saying rapidly, 'Right! I've got a few urgent phone calls to make while you pack. You'll see your father again at the hospital when he gets back to Brisbane.'

The last glimpse a now slightly hysterical Jodi saw of her father showed her his absolute amazement as his mouth opened and he began to protest in a furious voice, 'But. . .but you can't just. . .' and then Scott had whisked her out of earshot and literally bundled her into her room.

'You don't have to take me to Brisbane, Scott,' she protested faintly. 'I can go back with him.'

'And have him tear strips off you all the way? No way! I'll take you. There also may be something I can do for David and Ann.'

'But you don't even know them very well!'

'I know you, don't I? Or do I? I wonder!' His voice sounded bitter, and he added angrily, 'You'd better pack as quickly as you can. Anything you leave behind I can get to you later.' He was so abrupt that she was silenced, staring after him as he strode away without looking at her once.

So this was it. She looked around the room with sad eyes. Her last day in this house. Suddenly she recognised what a haven this had been for such a brief period. Her legs gave way, and she sank on to the bed. Jimmy and his family! In hospital! The ready tears sprang to her eyes again.

A moment later she could hear the angry voice of her father protesting loudly. Then there was the deep, decisive tones of Scott. A door clicked shut, and Jodi started automatically moving around the room collecting her belongings.

Some time later, she heard her father's harsh tones again, then what sounded like more furious protests. The front door slammed shut, and all was silent.

Jodi stood perfectly still until she heard the sound of a car revving away with a spurt of gravel. Then something deep inside her that was rigid and tense eased with relief. She released a deep breath, and started to pack.

It was in the comfortable white Mercedes that they started off for Brisbane, Scott insisting on driving. In fact, he managed so well that Jodi suspected that he had been capable of managing without her assistance for some time. He must have just wanted her with him. A little glow eased some of her hurt and confusion.

After they had been travelling for a short distance, Jodi ventured to ask him if her father had told him any more about the accident.

Scott snorted. 'Not much. He was too busy trying to convince me what an ungrateful, stupid pair of children he had fathered.'

'Oh!' Anger fought with hurt pride for dominance. 'And what did you have to say to that?' she snapped.

Scott didn't answer. His profile showed a rigid jaw, and his hands were clenched on the wheel.

'Besides telling him he was an overbearing idiot, nothing you need to know about. Yet, anyway,' he said curtly at last.

Jodi stared at him. She opened her mouth to protest, and then thought better of it. She subsided into silence.

On the way through Toowoomba, they called in briefly at the other surgery. Beyond telling Jodi curtly to wait in the car, Scott had said nothing about who had agreed to do the evening surgery at Wingeen for him.

There were four brass plates near the front entrance. It was a large building, and Jodi was surprised. Nothing Scott had said had given her the impression that the practice was as large and prosperous as it obviously was.

She guessed he had left one of his notes for Liz on the fridge door, but he had been so abrupt as they had left the house that she had known he was still angry. A deep hollow feeling inside her told her that for some reason he was really angry, furiously angry, with her. She almost cringed away from hearing him put that anger into words.

They talked very little the rest of the trip. Scott remained abrupt and grim. Jodi felt tongue-tied by the bleakness in his eyes whenever he looked at her. Once again, waves of exhaustion began sweeping through her, and despite her deep anxiety for her brother and his family, as well as her whole future, she found herself dozing off a couple of times. But there was still far too much time to think by the time they had reached the Royal Brisbane Hospital.

Jodi was almost faint with relief to discover that her brother had been transferred to the ward from the intensive care unit. A great part of that relief was not having again to be in such a unit with all the monitoring machines and paraphernalia, not to mention the atmosphere that always seemed to hover in such a place.

There were far too many bad memories it would have triggered off.

As used as she was to seeing how injuries to the head could distort a person's appearance, she still felt shocked when she saw David's swollen, bruised face. Scott's hand clasped her arm and steadied her as they approached the bed.

To her enormous relief, David opened his eyes and peered at them. 'Why, Sis, good to see you,' he said faintly. 'So the old man found you after all. Where've you been? Never seen him in such a tizz!'

Anger whelmed up in Jodi at this further evidence of her father's utter self-centredness. How dared he worry a sick man such as David with all of that?

'Oh, Jimmy, dear,' Jodi said tearfully as she reached for one of his hands, 'I came to take you up on your offer of a haven. The cablegram must still be sitting at the post office. But. . .how are you?'

He waved his free hand to and fro slightly. 'Only so-so yet. Thumpin' headache, and back's sore still.' He looked at Scott. 'Good heavens! Aren't you Dr Campbell?'

Scott nodded silently as Jodi said quickly, 'Scott came to my rescue when you didn't turn up at the airport,' and then was annoyed with herself at the anxious look that entered her brother's eyes. 'But I've been fine, Jimmy. Scott's been looking after me,' she hastened to say. 'It's you and Ann and Angela I'm worried about.'

'Oh, I'm all right,' he dismissed quickly. His eyes softened as he examined her. 'It sure feels good hearing you call me Jimmy again.'

Then his eyes clouded with worry and fear. 'Have you seen Ann and Angie yet?' he demanded, 'All

Father does is shrug and say they're fine. Apparently Ann's broken leg is in a temporary traction. But. . . but I. . .I'm so worried about them,' muttered David. 'Everyone keeps telling me they're doing all right, but I. . .' He stopped and swallowed. 'I don't know if it's only to keep me quiet, and they won't tell me the truth. . .or. . .or. . .' His voice had begun to rise fretfully.

Scott interrupted. 'What if we go and see them for you, and then come straight back and tell you how they are?'

'As long as you tell me the truth!'

'We will, Jimmy. . .or rather, David,' Scott's voice was firm and authoritative. 'Come on, Jodi, let David have a short rest. We'll be back as soon as we can.'

She reluctantly let go of her brother's hand and allowed Scott to escort her from the room, her fingers curling tightly and automatically around the warmth of his strong hand.

She let Scott ask for further directions, only nodding in total agreement when he said, 'We'll go and see your niece first. I suspect her mother will be as anxious about her as her father is.'

Jodi had not seen Angela for nearly two years, and then only briefly when they had called in to see her. The little blonde mite looked up suspiciously at them as they stopped beside her bed. Her face began to crumple, and she cringed away further under the bed-clothes.

'I'm Aunty Jodi, darling,' Jodi said swiftly, battling the tears that were forming rapidly in her own eyes, 'I'm your daddy's sister.'

Two tear-drenched blue eyes searched Jodi's face,

and then suddenly a small body catapulted itself across the bed and into Jodi's arms.

'Oh, Aunty Jodi. . .where's my mummy and daddy? Are they deaded?' the little girl wailed, bursting into noisy sobs.

'No, no, darling, of course not!' a shocked Jodi exclaimed as she hugged Angela tightly. 'They're being looked after in another ward.'

For a moment horror touched her at the realisation that she so easily might have not been able to reassure the tiny girl. She knew far too well how fragile life was in motor-vehicle accidents.

A harried-looking nurse appeared. 'Oh, are you relatives?' she asked breathlessly with obvious relief. 'Thank goodness! She's been so upset since her grandfather went this morning. If you are, Sister wants to see you.'

Jodi looked helplessly up at Scott as the little arms tightened around her.

'I'll go,' he said, and smiled briefly at her, before accompanying the nurse out of the ward.

It was some time before he returned. Jodi suspected, and had confirmed later, that he was making extensive enquiries about the three patients. He was accompanied by the sister, but his face was grim. A smile lightened it for Angela as she peered up at him from Jodi's lap.

'How about you come and see how your mum and dad are for yourself, Miss Muffet?' he said lightly, reaching out and gently ruffling the fine blonde curls.

A lip quivered for a moment as Angie stared up at Scott suspiciously. Then the sudden transformation of the little wan face made Jodi fight back her tears again.

'Oh, yes, please! I told them and told them Mummy

and Daddy'd want to see me. I'm their precsush darlin'!' she beamed up at Scott triumphantly.

'But I told you we should wait until we get her doctor's written permission for her to leave the ward,' fussed the harried-looking Sister angrily, 'and her grandfather, Dr Banner, he said——'

'And I told you, Sister, that I'd take full responsibility,' Scott snapped arrogantly. 'I'll even put that in black and white for you, if you like?'

Something rose up in Jodi to meet the sudden challenge she saw in his eyes as he looked meaningfully at her.

'I'm sure Sister doesn't expect you to do that, Dr Campbell,' she said sweetly, rising at the same time and hoisting Angela carefully up in her arms, careful not to bump the bandaged area on her little leg.

The woman's face cleared like magic. 'Oh, you're a *doctor*! Why on earth didn't you say so? I'm sure that makes it perfectly acceptable, as long as you go with them, sir,' she added hastily.

'I wouldn't dream of letting them out of my sight,' Scott growled. 'Here, I'll carry you, Miss Muffet. You're too big a girl for Aunty Jodi.'

To Jodi's wry flash of amusement, Angela let go of Jodi without hesitation as Scott reached for her. He certainly knew how to charm when he wanted to.

'My names not Mis' Muff. . . Muffet, silly.' Angie even gave a little giggle as she slipped an arm around his neck. 'She's in a story! I'm Angie!'

'But you look like her with all those gorgeous blonde curls,' teased Scott as he ruffled them again.

Jodi couldn't take her eyes off them as they established instant rapport. Angie snuggled her head down on his chest with a relieved sigh.

He cared so much for people that anyone that didn't want to be held in those strong arms would have to be a fool, Jodi told herself as she remembered how she had done the very same thing only the previous week.

Sister's smile slipped a little when Scott turned and scowled at her again. He lifted his chin and stared arrogantly down at the now flustered woman. No one in their right mind would defy that look, thought Jodi with a touch of amusement.

'Well, then, I suppose that's all right, then,' the agitated woman said reluctantly. 'Just make sure Angela doesn't run around on that injured leg of hers. And we're still keeping an eye on her for delayed shock.' Sister managed to sound in charge still, and then turned and scurried away.

'Stupid woman!' Scott muttered as they walked along the corridor. 'I couldn't believe they hadn't already made arrangements for this child to be taken to her parents! Too scared of your father! I insisted she ring Ann's ward and check if she was well enough for a visit from her daughter. At least the woman there jumped at the idea.'

They were met at the doorway of the women's ward by a bright-looking young sister who greeted them with, 'Oh, you darlings. I'm so glad you've brought her. I've been trying for days to——' She broke off with a short laugh, suddenly realising how indiscreet she was being.

It was Jodi's turn to frown when Scott turned on all his charm as he beamed at the sister approvingly. 'Ah, a very sensible and capable nurse! A visit from a patient's child is worth far more than all the medicines combined!' he exclaimed.

The bright young thing actually blushed. Jodi felt

jealousy rip through her. She moved past them.

'Which is Mrs Banner's room, please, Sister?' she asked crisply.

'First door on your right,' she was told just as crisply.

And, of course, Scott was perfectly right. A very tearful mother and daughter were reunited triumphantly. Despite her leg being suspended in traction, and one arm in plaster, Ann pulled Angie across the bed and hugged her tightly.

'Oh, I've been pesting the daylights out of them to bring her to me,' Ann said thankfully after she had greeted them, clutching Angie to her, and beaming up at them through her tears.

'An' I've been tellin' and tellin' 'em you'd want to see me,' said Angie indignantly.

'What's my granddaughter doing in here?' snapped a loud voice behind them. 'I told that ward sister in Paediatrics she wasn't ready for this kind of excitement yet!'

'I was wondering when you'd get here,' Jodi heard Scott mutter as her father stormed into the room.

Angie's face unexpectedly lit up as she saw him. 'There you are, Grandie. I told you I wanted to see my mummy, and this nice man broughted me!'

The transformation that took place on her father's face astounded Jodi as he looked at his granddaughter.

'I'm. . .I'm glad you're happy, then, darling,' he said lovingly.

A lump lodged in Jodi's throat. She could never remember her father ever looking at herself like that. He had never allowed either of his offspring to call him anything but Father either!

'But what about my daddy?' Angie asked anxiously. She turned and patted Ann's face with her little hand.

Ann looked up at Scott and Jodi. 'You just said you've already seen him, and he's still improving?' she asked them anxiously.

'Of course he is,' Dr Banner said impatiently. 'I told you that this morning.'

Ann's eyes, so much like her daughter's, were cool as she looked at him. 'So you did,' she said abruptly. 'But you were also insisting you couldn't stay in Brisbane any longer, and——' She stopped, glancing at Angie and then glaring at him silently.

Jodi's heart sank. Surely her father wasn't trying to throw his weight around here with her sister-in-law.

'I want to see my daddy, too!' Big tears had begun rolling down Angie's cheeks.

Her grandfather took a hasty step towards her, but Scott was there before him.

'Your daddy very much wants to see you too, sweetheart, but we'll have to make sure he's well enough first.'

Her eyes widened with fear. 'But you said he was only sleeping, Grandie! Is my daddy hurted bad?'

'Now see what you've done!' muttered the older man.

Scott ignored him. He reached out and pushed a curl back from the little pale forehead. 'He had a big bump on his head that made him sleep for a long time, but now he's awake. His face is hurt a bit too, and you would need to be very gentle with him. Do you think you could give him a very, very gentle kiss when you go and see him, and not bounce on the bed?'

With her eyes wide, the solemn little face nodded energetically at him. 'Can I show him the hurt on my leg an' let him kiss it better?'

'Of course, darling,' said Jodi in a shaky voice. 'Let's

go now. He said he wants to make sure you're all right, too.'

'And. . .and you tell him Mummy's only got a sore arm and leg, and I'll see him as soon as I can,' Ann said with a trembling smile, fighting to hold back her tears.

It was Scott again whom Angie held up her arms to, and Scott who carried her along the long corridors. Jodi had been very thankful that her father had elected to stay and show Ann what he had brought back for her.

Scott paused outside David's room. He looked significantly at Jodi as he hesitated.

She said quickly to Angie, 'Now remember, darling, Daddy's going to look a bit sick. He's going to take longer than you to be all better again. His face is hurt, but you must try and not let him see you crying, because he wants to make sure you are all right, too. So, can you give him a big smile, do you think?'

Angie nodded solemnly again, but she looked apprehensive.

'What about giving me a big practice smile?' coaxed Scott. He grinned at the little girl. 'You looked a very beautiful young lady when you smiled before.'

Angie smiled at him shyly.

'Lovely, simply lovely.' Scott beamed back at her, and stepped through the door as Jodi pushed it open for them.

And so the first sight David had of his precious daughter was as she gave a little giggle at Scott. Jodi felt the tears start down her own cheeks as she saw the absolute relief and adoration that lit up his poor battered face.

Scott gestured to Jodi to sit on the chair beside the bed, and, when she was seated, handed Angie to her.

Angie behaved beautifully. Her eyes were huge at the first sight of the swollen face, but with Jodi watching carefully she gave her father a gentle kiss, and was quite happy to cling to his hand. The man obviously relaxed as she chattered away happily to him about her mother, and then told him Aunty Jodi was just like her photo.

David glanced at Jodi with a slight smile at that, and then his eyes looked puzzled. Jodi had not dreamt he would make sure his little daughter would be made so familiar with his sister, and her amazed delight must have been evident.

Sudden understanding and compassion reached out to her from him. 'You're her one and only aunty, Jo, love. And I'll *always* be very proud of my special little sis.'

They stared at each other lovingly for a moment. Jodi heard Scott stir beside her and looked up at him. He was watching them with a strange expression. It almost looked like envy, she thought as her heart gave an unexpected leap.

Then his expression changed as she stared at him, and he said quietly to David, 'Your doctor will have a piece of me if we make you too tired, and so will the children's ward dragon sister if we keep this young lady away too long.'

David did look as though he was ready for another rest. He nodded reluctantly up at him, and Scott added cheerfully, 'Well, Angie, your mum's waiting for you to tell her all about Daddy now. So, we'd better hurry back to her.'

'Thank you, you two,' David murmured up at them both, his eyes full of emotion. 'I might be able to sleep properly now.'

As soon as they entered Ann's room again, they knew something had gone badly wrong since they had left. Ann's face was flushed with anger, and her father-in-law's face was full of grim determination.

CHAPTER ELEVEN

SCOTT took in the situation at a glance. 'We've come to tell you very quickly that our visit was a great success, but this little bundle needs a sleep.'

Ann bit her lip tightly as Angie was given a last hug. Angie smothered her mother's face with kisses, protesting loudly that she could stay with her and have a sleep.

'Now, Angie,' said her grandfather gently, with a significant look at Ann, 'your mother can't possibly look after you herself with her sore arm and leg.'

The tears threatened again in the blue eyes, and he said quickly, 'I'll take you back and tell you some more stories for a while. You can come back another time,' he added reluctantly, as rebellion still showed in the threatening tears and pouting little face. He avoided all the adult faces as he picked up Angie and strode from the room.

'I don't think I really believed all that David told me about his father until the last couple of days,' Ann said furiously into the silence that fell after the ward door swung closed. 'How could I believe such a well-known, successful surgeon could be so manipulative, so utterly selfish, so. . .so. . .?'

'So lonely?' Scott's voice was very quiet.

Both women looked at him in surprise.

Jodi thought about all the beautiful people that her father had surrounded himself with for as long as she could remember, even when her mother was alive. She had accepted years ago that he had needed them for satisfying some need in him for constant admiration, even adulation. It was when his own son and then his daughter had refused to be his puppets that he had shown them another side of his nature—a petty, vindictive side.

A sudden fear for Angie chilled Jodi. Perhaps he was lonely for family. But, whatever the reason, it had been very obvious that he had now turned his attentions to his granddaughter—but how would he try to manipulate her over the years? Well, both Jimmy and herself would be wide awake now to his devious tactics, she determined fiercely.

'If he is lonely, it's his own fault,' snapped Jodi unsympathetically. 'What's he up to now, Ann?'

'He says he has operations booked and appointments he can't postpone any longer. And he insists he has to take Angie back to Sydney with him so she will be properly cared for!' rattled off Ann desperately. 'He reminded me that it will be weeks before I'm back on both feet and my arm is of use again to be able to look after an active child. He knows I have no family in the Eastern States who can help out, and he says he can afford to employ a nanny and——'

'Utter garbage!' said Jodi fiercely. 'What does he think I'm going to do while all this is going on?'

Hope lit up Ann's eyes, but then it dimmed. 'I told him I was sure you would help us, but he stated you weren't well enough or capable enough, that you'd already failed miserably twice, and no way would he allow you to look after *his* granddaughter!'

Jodi was horror-stricken. It was true. She had failed twice. Professionally, and badly. He had known about the first time, and now someone must have told him about. . .

She stared helplessly at Ann, and then looked across her bed at the still figure of Scott.

His eyes locked with hers. Once again it seemed to Jodi as though he was searching out every nook and cranny in her soul and spirit. She waited for him to say something, to tell Ann he knew she would be able to cope. Hadn't she been coping extremely well this past week despite all that had happened?

Then she remembered the conversation that the arrival of her father had interrupted. She slumped in her chair, and looked back in confusion at Ann. Scott thought she needed counselling, needed to spill out her guts to someone. And deep down she knew he was right. There was so much she had to sort out deep inside her.

'Jodi?' His deep murmur reached her.

Her eyes flashed back to his face. She watched him rise from his chair and approach her. He stared down at her for another moment, the expression on his face impossible to decipher. Then he suddenly pulled her to her feet until she was touching him.

'Well, Jodi, do you think you can cope with an active four-year-old, and then her mother and father until they are completely fit again?'

As she stared at him, her self-esteem was at the lowest ebb it had ever been. Her lips trembled helplessly in despair.

His quiet yet forceful voice continued very quietly, very challengingly, 'A woman who survived a guerrilla attack in Africa——'

She started, opening her mouth in astonishment at his knowledge, but he tightened his grip on her hand

and she was silenced as he continued even more forcefully, his eyes filling with the tenderness and compassion she had learnt to look for.

'A woman who forced herself to help out with three emergencies within twenty-four hours when she probably should have been in hospital herself, a woman who stitched up a bullet wound after suffering trauma again herself, a woman whom not one of my patients doesn't admire and respect, a woman who even bowled over a hard nut like Liz in two minutes flat. . .can such a woman now stand up to her father again and tell him she can do whatever she has to?'

Jodi stared in absolute wonder up at him. Both had completely forgotten Ann as they stared at each other. Jodi's hand started to rise to touch his dear face.

'Oh, Jodi,' she heard Ann say with a sob, 'of course you could cope. And David and I wouldn't be completely useless.'

A flash of pure happiness flooded Jodi. Suddenly she felt more light-hearted than she had for many, many years, perhaps more than she ever had.

She took a deep breath, still not looking away from the searching expression in Scott's dark, dark eyes. 'Yes, Ann, of course I'll stay. As long as you need me.'

Scott's face changed again and he murmured, 'Atta girl!' as he had once before, but this time he moved the last few inches and kissed her gently, lovingly, on her lips.

Familiar fire raged through her, but he released her abruptly and turned to Ann. 'Right.' He took a deep breath, and one hand raked through his hair. 'Some practical issues. Have you been given any idea how long you'll be in here?'

Ann looked disgruntled. 'You doctors are all alike. You smile vaguely, and just say you'll wait and see. When they set my arm a few days ago——'

Jodi gasped. 'A few days ago! But Father said. . .'

'Exactly,' said Scott abruptly. 'That's what the sister in Angie's ward told me. The accident happened five days ago.'

'But he said Jimmy had only just regained consciousness!'

'Your father didn't actually say that, he really only implied it had just happened, but he clearly wanted us to believe your brother had just regained consciousness.'

'David regained his senses twenty-four hours after the accident,' stated Ann firmly. She looked worried again. 'But apparently he's hurt his back, and isn't allowed out of bed.'

'But there was absolutely no reason why Angie could not have been reunited with her parents days ago! No reason you two adults could not even be sharing the same room!' Scott said furiously, his eyes flashing with disgust.

'Oh, yes, there was a good reason, though,' Ann said bitterly.

'Father,' Jodi said through gritted teeth.

'Apparently he used to know the head honcho here from way back. And I am very much looking forward to my consultant orthopaedic surgeon's next visit!' Ann said fiercely. 'I only found out today after my dear father-in-law left for Kingsluck. I know now he only insisted on going because he's brought most of Angie's clothes and some of her toys back so he can take them to Sydney with him!'

'Hmm,' said Scott, tapping his fingers thoughtfully

on the bed, and then looking at the doctor's name on the card above the bed. 'How come you and your husband are in private rooms?'

'My father-in-law insisted!'

'And your orthopod? Does he by any chance hold a big position here?'

Jodi was beginning to know what Scott was thinking, and wasn't at all surprised when Ann said grimly, 'The head honcho!'

'Right!' said Scott again. 'And you're not completely satisfied with your treatment by him?'

Ann's eyes widened, and then narrowed as she thought about that.

'If you're not satisfied, you can always ask for a second opinion,' Jodi said softly, grasping immediately what Scott was thinking, 'even change doctors.'

'I have to say he does have the reputation of being a very good doctor,' Scott warned them both, 'and it would be a shame actually to change at this stage. I think perhaps a slight hint that you are thinking of doing so may be sufficient,' he added, a slight twinkle lighting up his eyes mischievously.

So it was that when Dr Banner strode into the room a few moments later he was considerably taken back by the smiles that were on their faces. He was more then taken back when Ann immediately informed him calmly that Jodi was only too willing to stay and look after them all.

'No way will I allow Angie to go to Sydney,' she finished emphatically.

His face began to look mottled with rage. 'Don't be stupid, woman——' he started to say furiously.

'As you know, I only live a few kilometres away,' Scott interrupted haughtily, at his most professional.

'They are *my* patients, and, of course, I'll be keeping the closest eye on them all.'

Dr Banner drew himself up and glared at him. 'They are not your patients while they are in this hospital, young man, and. . .'

'And neither are they yours, sir,' Scott said in his steeliest voice, 'and Ann and David are Angela's legal next of kin,' he added steadily.

'And although my doctor here may be an old friend of yours, I'm not entirely happy with his treatment, and I've almost decided to change doctors,' Ann threw in.

'And Dr Campbell is also my doctor, and whom I'm working for at present. He has just told me that it's his professional opinion that I'm more than capable of looking after them all.' Jodi drew herself up very straight, very proudly, and stared back at the even more angry, and now outnumbered man.

A few moments later, the three were alone again. Dr Banner was no fool, and knew when he was defeated. He had not left gracefully however. After giving everyone his opinion of his worthless son and stubborn daughter-in-law, he had turned on Jodi.

'And don't think you can ever come sneaking back home, young lady,' he had said with tight lips and a flushed, furious face. 'With the type of nurse you've proved to be, it's just as well you never did try medicine! I'll see that all of the rest of your things are packed up and sent to you, and you can wait until you're invited to my house in the future!' Then he had turned on his heel, and stormed off.

Now that he'd gone, Jodi started trembling, and then felt Scott's hand rest on her shoulder. He squeezed it in silent comfort as he murmured with a hint of amusement, 'We should be thankful he's so willing to preserve his hospital image by not yelling like he did at Wingeen.'

Ann sank back on her pillows. She looked exhausted.

'Ann,' said Scott softly, 'we'll leave you to rest in a moment, but just one more thing. My aunt Dorothy lives here in Brisbane, and has already agreed for Jodi to stay with her. Would you be happy about your daughter going there with her until you're allowed home to Kingsluck? I've already spoken to the paediatrician in charge of her, and he says she's ready for discharge as soon as arrangements can be made.'

Jodi stared at Scott. Would this man never cease to astound her with his forethought, and his knowing instinctively what was so desperately needed?

After Ann had agreed without protest, they said their goodbyes and left her to rest. Outside in the corridor, Jodi turned to Scott, and clutched his arm.

'I don't know how we're ever going to thank you, Scott,' she said tearfully.

'You may not be thanking me after a few days being bossed around by Aunt Dorothy,' he said with a faint smile, but Jodi noticed that it didn't reach his eyes this time, and the dimple stayed hidden.

She drew back, rebuffed and a little puzzled. Was he for some reason regretting her getting involved with his family?

'How. . .?' She swallowed as they started walking swiftly, 'How long do you think it'll be before Ann and David will be allowed home? She only has a Hamilton Russells traction, so. . .'

'So it must be a temporary one to counteract muscle spasms in her thigh muscles, and until the swelling goes down,' Scott continued for her when she hesitated. 'I'd say in the next day or so she'll have an intramedullary nail inserted in her femur, but she'll find it difficult even partially weight-bearing for a few weeks. With that arm in a cast, she won't be able to use crutches or a walker. But let's get you settled at Aunt Dorothy's now, and you'll be able to sort that out tomorrow.'

Conversation, once they were in the close confines of the car, once again dried up. Jodi glanced a couple of times at Scott's closed, grim face, and wondered miserably if he was already regretting involving his aunt in her problems.

They drove north for about twenty minutes, and it was almost dark by the time they turned off the Bruce Highway. They passed a sign for Bridgeman Downs, and Jodi sat up straighter as she realised they were driving past some beautiful homes set well back from the road. Then they turned into a well-lit, tree-lined avenue and stopped at the entrance to a huge red brick home.

Belatedly, she remembered that Liz had at no time given the impression that she was one of the usual run-of-the-mill poverty-stricken university students. Jodi was no stranger to the luxurious lifestyle of her father over the past few years, but, even so, she was taken back by this imposing residence.

In a sudden panic, she turned to Scott. 'I didn't dream your aunt's place would be anything like this! Are you sure——?'

'Of course I am,' he said impatiently as he held her door open. 'Let's get inside. I don't know about you but I'm starving.'

Dorothy Campbell was an older version of her daughter. Even the slightly outrageous outfit she was wearing was reminiscent of Jodi's first meeting with Liz. She welcomed Scott with a big hug, and surveyed Jodi for a moment through narrowed eyes.

Then a very familiar, mischievous twinkle lit her eyes as she took a step forward and suddenly enveloped Jodi too with a hug and kiss on the cheek.

'Well, there's no doubt about that daughter of mine,' she said cryptically, 'She's right again!'

Jodi wasn't quite sure why, but she felt a blush start to heat her face. Before she could speak, Scott gave a snort.

'Knowing Liz, she's probably very wrong,' he drawled wearily.

Dorothy's expression altered as she looked back at him. 'You're both very tired, my dears. Have you had anything to eat?' Scott shook his head silently, and she said brightly, 'Right, your rooms first, and while you freshen up I'll dish up.'

Only then did Jodi realise that Scott was staying too. 'Oh,' she blankly, 'don't you have to get back for the morning insulins?'

And then she felt confused as he suddenly grinned at her. 'Spoken like a true nurse, Jodi!' His eyes suddenly shone with tenderness, and her heart turned over. 'And what would you do if I said I'd forgotten all about them?' he teased her.

'Not believe you,' she shot back, and then knew her face became scarlet as Dorothy suddenly chuckled.

'More and more I give Liz credit for being astute,' she murmured. They both swung towards her, but she suddenly became all bustling efficiency.

In a very short space of time she had shown them to their adjoining bedrooms, and disappeared, leaving Jodi to look around her large, comfortable room still wondering what on earth Liz had told her mother about her relationship with Scott.

CHAPTER TWELVE

IT MIGHT have been a very beautiful, luxurious home, but by the time Jodi and Scott had been served a simple, nourishing meal cooked and served by Dorothy herself Jodi felt more at home than she had been for a long, long time at her father's house.

And that's what it is now, she thought sadly, my father's house. I don't really have a home any more.

As she thought about the future, Jodi didn't realise how silent she became as they finished their meal. It was more than time she thought of buying her own home. Although her trip to Africa had taken a little of it, she had been able to save a nice little nest-egg over the years, and it would do for a deposit on a modest house somewhere. But where? And would she be able to find another job?

'Jodi, don't worry about tomorrow, now,' Scott's gentle tones intruded.

She looked up with a start, and realised that both Scott and Dorothy were watching her with understanding and sympathy. Scott had been talking to his aunt when she had entered the dining-room, and knew he must have told her some of what had happened at the hospital.

'Oh, I'm. . .I'm sorry. . .' she stammered. She quickly put down the spoon she had been unconsciously toying with. 'And it wasn't just tomorrow. I was thinking about a whole new future I have to plan for after David and Ann no longer need help.'

'As Scott said, don't worry about any of your tomorrows, Jodi,' Dorothy said confidently. 'We're a big family, and we've found there's always a rainbow after our storms.'

'Yeah,' Scott drawled as he looked directly at his aunt. 'Our family's always been keen on helping the rainbows happen, too, hasn't it, dear Aunt?'

She looked discomfited for a moment, and then sprang hastily to her feet. 'Well, I'm afraid I have to go out for a while to one of those never-ending committee meetings, so I'll leave you two to clear away, if you wouldn't mind?'

Jodi and Scott obediently cleared away and loaded the dishwasher, before Scott led the way into a comfortable family-room.

'Want to watch TV for a while, or shall I put on a CD?' Scott asked quietly.

Jodi hesitated, and then took a deep breath. 'I. . .I think we need to talk, Scott,' she said unsteadily. 'My father said some things today, and he no doubt told you other things about me that——'

'I'm not at all interested in what your father said,' Scott interrupted. 'And there's something I should tell you too, but I'll put on some music first, I think. What would you like, classical or classical?'

A faint smile twitched Jodi's lips. 'As long as it's not too heavy, I don't mind a little classical, but I love musical comedies.'

He pulled a face at her, and said with a martyr's air, 'A compromise, then.'

As the orchestral sounds of Andrew Lloyd Webber's themes from his musicals softly started, Scott relaxed on a comfortable, slightly battered old chair opposite Jodi with a sigh.

'This place has almost been like a second home to me,' he murmured softly. 'We used to spend quite a few holidays here or at Edith's. But I haven't been able to come much for some years now.'

'You're a very close family, aren't you?' Jodi said huskily, in one way glad that he had chosen to sit so far away from her, and yet a little hurt that he had not joined her on the sofa.

He nodded confirmation. 'Your brother was very glad and relieved to see you today, Jodi, so why haven't you seen much of him over the years?'

Jodi shrugged. 'I'm not really sure that I know. We could certainly have done so these past few years since I've been independent of my father's money, but I guess by then the pattern was set. He's quite a bit older than me, and after Mum died and he decided that same year to drop medicine——'

'He was studying to be a doctor?' Scott interrupted with some surprise.

'Yes, he was in his second year when Mum got sick.' Her voice hardened. 'She had cancer and he. . .he dropped out to be with her. Father had been booked in to do a special course in London for several months, and refused to cancel it. Oh, he made sure she had a private nurse, and everything money could buy, but Mum only wanted someone there who loved her. She. . .she died before Father came home.'

'And you were only fourteen,' Scott murmured sympathetically.

She nodded slightly, remembering the time she had told him something about her family. 'After Mum died, he had a dreadful row with Father and moved out. He got a part-time job, because Father refused all financial support, and did his accountancy degree part-time.

When I got old enough we used to meet sometimes without Father knowing, but we did drift apart. He told me once that he'd only started medicine because Father had persuaded him to.'

'And so you defied your father, too.'

She gave a grim laugh. 'For more years than I like to think about. I don't think a year went by that he didn't think up some scheme to get me to change to being a doctor—after I became a registered nurse, after my midwifery course, my intensive-care course.'

'And so you kept on training, always trying to get him to approve of you, always putting yourself under more and more stress.'

She looked across at him in some surprise. He had been avoiding her eyes, his head resting back on his folded hands and staring into space. Now he moved, and their eyes locked again. It was Jodi who looked away first.

'Even six months ago you were thoroughly exhausted, weren't you?' he persisted.

Jodi stared into space, thinking of that dreadful time leading up to then. Once again her father had been pressuring her to apply. This time he 'knew someone who knew someone, and she would be an absolute fool if. . .' and so it had gone on and on.

It was almost as though he had known this was a last-ditch attempt. Never had he been so persistent since that summer she had finished high school. Last year she had learnt to dread her off-duty times. He had turned up at her flat. He had rung her, left numerous messages on her answering machine. Through long practice she had been able to ignore him most of the time.

And then she had come down with a bad bout of

influenza. Even then he had not stopped pesting her. If anything it had been worse. It was an obsession with him. She had given in to his persuasion to stay in her old room at home to recuperate, but at last she had been driven back to her own flat, and even been foolish enough to go back to work too soon, mainly to escape him.

'What were the mistakes you made in IC, Jodi?'

'Mistake, as in singular, you mean,' Jodi said grimly. 'There was one in IC and. . .and another. . .in Africa. . .' She closed her eyes for a moment, trying to shut out the remembered horror of that last incident.

Scott frowned. 'According to your father, there were two mistakes when you were working in intensive care.'

'In IC?' She stared at Scott. She was silent for a moment, and then shrugged. 'No, you must have misunderstood him. There was only one mistake there. He must have found out about. . .' She paused, and then began slowly, 'But when did he. . .? Oh!' she said flatly. 'At Wingeen. No doubt he was trying to convince you I was unemployable.' Then her eyes widened. 'Two mistakes in IC? He. . .he said. . .'

Suddenly, rage flooded her. She sprang to her feet. 'That's a lie! It was *not* my fault!' Her hands clenched in two fists, she stared furiously at Scott. 'Just what did he tell you? That I tried to implicate and blame a doctor to cover myself? Is *that* why you've been so. . . so. . .withdrawn?'

Scott stared up at her, a startled expression crossing his face. Then he pushed himself slowly to his feet, and reached down and took one of her clenched fists into both of his.

'Calm down, sweetheart. It doesn't really matter what *he* told me. I want you to tell me yourself.'

It was the more familiar gentle, sympathetic Scott who urged her to sit down again, not the reserved man who had been in evidence since they had left the hospital. He didn't let go of her hand as he sat down beside her this time.

She was trembling, and took a deep breath. 'I think what upset me the most was that the. . .the RMO involved I had considered a very good friend,' she began.

She felt his hand tighten slightly on hers, and she added hastily, 'Oh, there was never anything more between Martin and me than a couple of dinner dates, and once we went to a daytime movie when our off-duties coincided. But I liked him, and I. . .I thought we were friends.'

Then she told him rapidly about the evening she had had to ring Martin to get him to re-order some more anti-hypertensive medication for a patient, because the day staff had neglected to do so. He had told her the consultant had wanted it re-assessed for the next dose. Then he had said hurriedly that he was due in Theatre and was unable to come there and then to write it up, and would have to make it a phone order.

Jodi had been a little surprised at the amount of the increased dosage, but had written it down, read it back to him, and then asked him to hold on while she asked another nurse to come to the phone so that he could also tell her, thus obeying the hospital's ruling for phone orders.

'Oh, Jodi, be a love, and don't bother anyone this time,' he had begged her hurriedly, 'I promise I'll be there straight after this case. Probably before its due, anyway.' Then he had rung off.

'I was annoyed with him,' she told Scott, 'but I

thought I knew him well enough to know he would come as soon as he could.' She gave a mirthless laugh. 'So I said a few things under my breath about the day staff, and RMOs in particular, and even left the patient's chart on the desk near the phone. The only "mistake" I made was not crossing out what I'd written.'

'And so someone gave the patient an incorrect dose,' Scott said thoughtfully, 'and you got the blame?'

'Did I get the blame!' Jodi said bitterly. 'According to my so-called friend, Martin, the whole thing was my fault. According to him he would never have ordered such a high dosage, and I had written it down incorrectly.'

She was silent, remembering how the director of nursing had still been furious with a thoroughly devastated Jodi, even though she had believed her IC nursing unit manager.

'But you were stupid enough not to obey the rules and insist that he repeat his phone order to another nurse,' she had stormed at Jodi. 'It doesn't matter how well we think we know a doctor, when it boils down to his career against a nurse's, he'll protect his every time! You were sensible enough not to return the chart to the bedside, but in the meantime another nurse grabbed the chart, and you were only very fortunate you didn't have a patient die as a result!'

Scott's hand touched her face. She looked at him with dry, burning eyes.

'But that's not the incident you think of when you think of the mistake you made?' he asked softly.

She closed her eyes, and turned her head away from his searching look.

'No,' she said curtly. 'We were fortunate that the

patient still had an arterial line having his BP being monitored. There was a bit of a panic, but *that* patient survived. It did have some bearing on what happened later, but it wasn't the reason I was forced to resign, or face charges and be dismissed.'

She felt Scott tense, and snatched her hand from his. She stood up, moving a little distance away and not looking at him.

'Shortly after returning from my interview the very next day, when I was reprimanded by the DON, I forgot that the new patient we had been expecting while I was out of the ward had the same surname as another admitted the previous day. I picked up the wrong chart, and gave the patient I knew a drug prescribed for the new admission. He died.'

Scott remained silent. Jodi ventured one swift glance at him, and her heart sank. He was scowling ferociously, and she knew he would have little sympathy for anyone who did that to one of his patients.

It had been such a stupid, basic thing that every nurse was warned about when they first started their training. So many people from the hospital had snubbed her afterwards, even fellow nurses she had once thought were good friends. Her father had expressed absolute abhorrence that a daughter of his could have made such a horrendous mistake. Everywhere she had turned she had only found condemnation.

Several weeks later she had thankfully flown off to Africa.

She heard Scott move, and held her breath. He turned her gently to face him. She looked desperately at him, frightened that this man she loved so desperately would also reject her.

'Am I right in thinking this happened when you were still upset about the phone order?' he said slowly, nothing but deep compassion in his face.

She nodded jerkily. 'Just after I returned from the DON's office.'

'Was there actually an inquest into the death, Jodi?'

That was something she had been a little surprised about, but so relieved that she had not thought about it very much. She shook her head numbly.

He looked surprised, and then unexpectedly smiled at her. 'A bit of a cover-up, was there?'

'Y-yes. . .' she stammered after a moment of sheer astonishment, 'Yes. . . I. . .I suppose you could call it that, although the consultant in charge of that patient actually rang me and told me he believed the patient had no chance of surviving anyway, even if. . .'

Scott's smile spread. 'I thought so! If a high-and-mighty consultant actually took the time out to contact you, and you were allowed to resign, you must have been one excellent sister! Even high-and-mighty consultants make mistakes, and I guess lofty nursing unit managers are allowed to also if there are extenuating circumstances.'

He was speaking rapidly. She opened her mouth to protest, but he added before she could speak, 'By forcing you to resign, I bet the nursing hierarchy were covering themselves as well because of that other unfortunate episode with the phone order. I wouldn't be at all surprised if your friend Martin got an almighty blast from his boss, who probably didn't believe him either! It *would* have looked bad if nursing admin hadn't been seen to discipline you after an apparent second mistake, in the event of an enquiry some-time in the future!' he finished triumphantly.

Jodi gaped at him. She wasn't sure if she went along with his reasoning, but it was the first time anyone had even tried to make excuses for her.

'Well,' he said a little impatiently, 'what do you think? I'm right, aren't I?'

Jodi didn't have a clue whether he was or not. All she knew was that this man—this beloved man—was not only making excuses, but somehow minimising what until now had been a dreadful episode in her life. Helpless tears crept into her wide eyes, and spilled slowly over.

Suddenly it seemed so natural to feel his arms wrap around her, and she leaned into him, hungry for the safety she instinctively knew was in his solid strength. And Jodi, for perhaps the first time in her life, felt protected, cared for, as though nothing bad could ever happen to her while this wonderful man held her tightly.

'I could quite easily get addicted to cuddling you like this,' a soft voice whispered in her ear, 'and I think I'll have to kiss you very, very soon, even if you still haven't finished talking.'

Jodi froze. For one incredible moment she had been desperate to feel again his well-shaped, full lips on hers, but she had still to tell him about the other mistake.

And she had to tell him. All of it. She tried to pull back. His arms tightened for a moment, but then he let her go. She stumbled back a little too fast, and his arms caught hers to steady her.

'I. . .I. . .you've been very kind,' she managed a little breathlessly, 'but I haven't finished yet.'

The flame in the eyes looking into hers dimmed, and then his arms dropped away. 'Kind!' he rasped, turning away. 'Well, finish, then.'

She saw him take a couple of deep breaths. He sank on to the sofa again, and patted the seat beside him invitingly.

'No,' she said nervously, 'I'd rather stand. I. . . I. . .' She walked shakily away a few paces, and then turned. 'Would. . .would you like a cup of tea?' she asked nervously.

'For goodness' sake, why don't you just finish confessing all your supposed dreadful crimes and get it over with?' he growled suddenly.

'Supposed!'

'Oh, come on, Jodi,' he said impatiently, beginning to scowl at her, 'you're a good nurse. Whatever you've done can't be that bad. This one must have happened overseas, right?'

Suddenly she was angry. How dared he dismiss the sleepless nights, the nightmares, as something that was relatively unimportant?

'Would you call infecting someone with HIV virus not that bad, then?' she suddenly yelled at him.

She saw him freeze, and all the colour disappeared from his face.

'Jodi, no!'

She saw his pale lips mouth the words, saw the absolute horror that filled him. Then he covered his face with his hands, and she heard the groan that ripped through him.

It was more than she could take. Her breath coming in gasps, she turned and fled.

He didn't follow her to her room, and she didn't hear him enter his own bedroom during the long hours of the night when she lay wide awake, staring hopelessly at the ceiling.

And in the morning Scott had gone.

CHAPTER THIRTEEN

It was fortunate for Jodi that Angie was discharged that very same day so that she was forced to think of something else besides Scott.

Dorothy had just told Jodi that Scott had apparently decided to go home early, only leaving a brief note, when the phone rang. The fact that Scott had returned very early to Wingeen, without saying goodbye, had hardly sunk in, as Dorothy spoke for a few moments into the phone in the kitchen before beckoning to Jodi.

'It's your sister-in-law, Ann,' Dorothy said briefly.

Jodi moved slowly, her limbs feeling like lead. Scott had gone. He had rejected her too.

She listened silently to Ann's excited voice. 'Oh, Jodi, Angie can go home with you today. When can you get here?'

Jodi swallowed, forcing back the lump in her throat.

'Jodi? Are you there?'

'Yes. . .yes, Ann, I'm here. I. . .'

There was a pause on the other end of the phone, and then Ann said hesitantly, 'Are you OK, Jodi? Is there some problem after all about Scott's aunt having you both?'

Jodi made a tremendous effort to pull herself together.

'Ann,' she said in a choked voice, 'can I get back to you? I'm not sure——'

Dorothy was suddenly beside her, and took the receiver from Jodi's limp hand.

'Ann, it's Dorothy Campbell. Is it your daughter? She can be discharged?'

Jodi listened in a haze of pain as Dorothy reassured Ann that they could stay with her, and told her she would drive Jodi to the hospital. Dorothy was brisk and businesslike, as managing as Scott in her own way.

She turned to Jodi after she had hung up, and said crisply, 'It's obvious you and Scott must have had a serious disagreement last night. But that's absolutely no reason why you still can't stay here until your family's well enough to go home. Now, have something to eat, and as soon as you're ready we'll go.' Her face softened as she looked at Jodi's devastated face. 'It'll all work out, dear. Just give it time.'

But in the days that followed without a word from Scott, Jodi knew Dorothy was wrong.

Fortunately, it was very distracting looking after a lively four-year-old, and taking her daily to the hospital to see her parents. But as the days dragged by, the ache that had settled in her heart continued to throb like an open wound.

To make it worse, there were several photographs of Scott around the house, constant reminders of his various expressions, his various moods. There was a much younger Scott in a large family group, a sun-tanned, laughing Scott hugging Liz, a serious, frowning Scott playing tennis.

During that first week, Dorothy reported cheerfully a couple of times that Scott had rung, but Jodi knew he always timed his calls for when she would be at the hospital.

He had been right about Ann having her leg operated on. The first Monday after Angie was discharged, Ann had been scheduled for theatre, and the metal rod called an intramedullary nail was inserted into the shaft of her fractured femur. And while she was kept in bed after that for the next week or so until the sutures were removed, David had been put into traction for his back.

So the weeks slipped by, and it was almost a month since the accident before both David and Ann were considered able to manage well enough to be allowed back to Kingsluck. Ann had gradually been able to partial weight-bear on her leg, but it had been very difficult with her arm still in plaster. She still had to resort to the wheelchair for any distances, and often by the end of the day was very weary.

In that time, Jodi gradually gave up hope of Scott contacting her again, and knew that somehow she would have to try and stop loving him. So many times in the past she had tried to comfort others by saying, as Dorothy had, that time would help to dull the pain of loss. How much time would she need? she wondered hopelessly in the darkness of the night hours. Forever?

When the great day came, Dorothy insisted on driving them all back to Kingsluck, stating that it was more than time she checked out what her daughter Liz was up to. They tumbled out of the car on a bleak, cold winter's morning, shivering as an icy westerly wind tried to penetrate their warm clothing, only adequate for Brisbane's milder coastal winter.

'Brr. . .' shivered Dorothy, 'I knew there was a good reason why I never come to the Darling Downs in the winter!'

David laughed as he moved slowly and cautiously, still in his spinal brace, to turn on the reverse-cycle air-conditioner to warm the house. 'It's cold all right, but boy. . .' he looked around with deep satisfaction '. . .it's great to be home!'

Despite their efforts, Dorothy refused to stay any longer than it took to unload the car.

'No, my dears,' she insisted cheerfully, 'you've got too much to sort out, and I want to call in at Wingeen and see Liz and Scott.'

Jodi went out to the car with her, and forced a smile as she said goodbye. 'I don't know how we can ever thank you,' she murmured as she gave Dorothy a big hug and kiss.

Dorothy snorted unexpectedly as she hugged Jodi back. 'I know how! Bring that big, stubborn nephew of mine to his senses! I don't want to lose a great girl like you from the family.'

Jodi waved her off dry-eyed. She had not been able to mention Scott easily, and no one had talked about him at all in her hearing lately. She was trembling slightly as she slowly entered her bedroom, and remembered the night he had shared her bed so innocently.

That evening Dorothy rang her. She sounded angry and frustrated.

'Jodi, I thought you should know that Scott's gone back to Sydney,' she said bluntly. 'Edith and Douglas arrived home unexpectedly a couple of days ago. Liz told me Scott up and said he had urgent business in Sydney he had put off long enough. Despite all their protests, he left. They're very put out that they've had no time to settle in before starting work again.'

Jodi walked slowly back to her room and closed her door. So he was really gone now, she thought hopelessly as she stared blindly before her. One part of her was very relieved that there would be no risk of accidentally bumping into him, the other part of her felt nothing but raw pain, and a sense of loss and bitter disappointment.

Somehow she had to start a new life, and forget him, she tried to tell herself firmly. It wouldn't be long before Ann's arm would be out of plaster and she would be back to full strength. Jodi would no longer be needed here.

As the tears flowed down her cheeks yet again, Jodi knew it would take her aeons of time, if ever, to recover from loving Scott.

The next morning she decided that she wouldn't mention anything to Ann and David about leaving and finding work as soon as possible, as she had intended. Now that Scott had gone, there was no point. There was nothing for her in Sydney any more. She would stay in Queensland wherever she could get work.

There had been plenty of time during the past weeks for Jodi to rest and relax, and physically she was much improved. If some mornings her mirror had told her there were dark shadows under her eyes, no one had commented, and she guessed that Dorothy had told David and Ann what she knew about her supposed row with Scott.

The very next afternoon, Jodi had a visitor. She was outside digging up a flowerbed ready for planting some spring annuals, despite her brother's protests, when the noise of a vehicle slowing down and turning into the drive made her pause and turn around.

The digging-fork fell from her suddenly nerveless hands at the sight of the familiar red Land Rover. As it pulled slowly to a stop, she let out her breath painfully. By the time the woman driving it had left the vehicle and advanced on her, Jodi was nervously pulling off her borrowed gardening gloves.

'Hello, you must be Jodi. I'm Edith Wallace,' the woman said directly.

As Jodi murmured an astonished greeting, she was aware of being studied carefully.

'I. . .I thought you'd be much older,' Jodi blurted out, and then felt colour rush to her face as the woman's face relaxed and her eyes began to twinkle.

'Well, what dire things did that nephew of mine tell you about me?' she said with a smile. 'Called me Aunty, I suppose, as though I'm much more than a mere seven years older than him. His mother is my eldest sister, and is eighteen years older than me.' The smile disappeared. 'Another thing I intend to rap him over the knuckles for. He pretty well left us in the lurch after we arrived home. Jodi, I've come to ask a favour of you.'

Jodi hesitated, and than reluctantly invited Edith inside out of the cold. She introduced her to Ann and David who were watching television in the lounge, and then led the way through to the kitchen.

'I hope you don't mind if we talk here,' Jodi said a little nervously. 'Would you like a drink?'

'Yes, please, I'd love a cup of tea,' said Edith fervently as she sat down with a sigh of relief. 'I've just finished the district run, and my muscles need to be toned up again after our extended holiday.'

'Scott. . . Scott said you were really on your honeymoon,' Jodi said quietly as she set about preparing afternoon tea, glad to have something to do with her hands.

'I wish I were still on that honeymoon, too. It was marvellous!' She beamed, and then frowned. 'I wish we were still away for more than one reason!' After a slight pause, she added grimly, 'in fact, we only came home to see how things were, intending to leave again for another couple of weeks in Brisbane with Doug's relatives, but Scott just up and went.

'Jodi,' she continued in a rush, 'I've had people asking after you today, as well as all day yesterday. Everyone keeps telling me what a good nurse you were. Would you like to take over my job as district nurse?'

Jodi put down the cup and saucer in her hand, and stared at Edith. Could this be the answer to her future? She had certainly enjoyed those days with Scott, no matter how reluctant she might feel about hearing his name referred to from time to time.

'I'm. . .I'm not sure,' she said slowly at last. 'Edith, did Scott ever tell you about. . .about why I gave up my job in Sydney?'

Edith looked at her steadily. 'As a matter of fact he did. Right after he told me he had virtually blackmailed you into helping him. He was very upset about that.'

Jodi looked blankly at her. 'Scott was upset? But he didn't blackmail me!'

'He said he made out his hand was a lot worse than it was to get you to accompany him on his rounds.'

'Oh!'

'He seemed to think you needed help regaining your self-confidence. Or that was his excuse, anyway.' Edith studied her for a moment, and then seemed to make up her mind about something.

'He found it difficult to talk about you at all. So much so, in fact, that I'm forced to agree with Liz. He fell for you hard. And, from what Dorothy has said, the feeling seems to have been mutual.'

Jodi stared at her, despair creeping into her voice

as she said vehemently, 'But he didn't fall for me hard enough to be able to accept me and the mistakes I've made!'

She turned away, hugging herself tightly, tears burning the back of her eyes. Edith was silent, and then she rose and moved to confront her.

'I still think the incident in Sydney doesn't wipe out the fact that you're a very competent, highly qualified nursing sister,' she said firmly, 'and on behalf of the local committee, whose chairman just happens to be my husband, by the way, I'm offering you a permanent position as the new district nurse.'

Jodi's eyes widened. 'But won't you be returning at all?'

A very satisfied, self-congratulatory smirk filled Edith's face. 'In seven months' time I'd have to leave anyway. I'm pregnant.' Her face was suddenly radiant, and a deep pang tore through Jodi. 'Douglas is apprehensive because I'm so old to be having our first, and he's laid down the law. No work, as of now!'

'I'm so very glad for you,' Jodi said huskily. She took a deep breath, and took the plunge. 'I'd be very glad to take over your job.'

Edith breathed a sigh of relief. 'You won't have to worry about assisting at the surgery for a few months. I should be able to manage that for Douglas at least. Thank goodness I won't have to bend over and thump our Beth. . .' She paused, then said with a rush, 'Can you possibly start tomorrow? Morning sickness has struck, and Douglas has even done the early insulins the past couple of days, and moaned loudly about it, too. We can fix up the paperwork when you finish tomorrow afternoon.'

And so, early the next morning, still finding it difficult to believe that her immediate future had been settled so speedily, Jodi drove David's car over to Wingeen. The plan was for her to be supplied with a vehicle eventually, but for the time being she would use the Land Rover. Edith was waiting for her, and went through the list of patients with her before she set off.

What she should have thought of was the number of times the patients on her list wanted to talk about Scott!

Mr Wilson, the old man with lung cancer, was still visiting his daughter. He was now too weak to shower himself, and had reluctantly submitted at last to help from the nurse, Edith had told her.

He was notably thinner and even more breathless, but he still managed to give a brief, knowing cackle, and to leer at her.

'Very down in the mouth, 'e was, the doc,' he said between noisy gasps. 'Snapped me 'ead off. Only asked where ya was! 'ad a fight, did ya?'

By then, Jodi had to bite her own tongue to prevent herself from snapping back! But she just managed a brief, vague smile which she knew hadn't fooled him one scrap, as she continued helping him to dress. He gave another cackle that was cut off in the middle by a coughing attack. After that he was too breathless to do more than rest in his reclining chair, and wave his hand at her as she quietly said goodbye.

She had a heart-warming welcome from Beth Field, but she also raved on about Scott, until Jodi felt thoroughly drained. The list of patients had grown during the past few weeks and she was very weary by the end of the day, as much from fending off comments about Scott's departure as from the actual work involved.

The days fell into a pattern after that, and Jodi found that the old satisfaction she had found in caring for people years before had returned. She enjoyed having the weekends off to spend with her family, and began to realise just how tiring continual shift work for so many years, with its disturbed sleeping patterns, had been.

With the strength of character that had helped her to stand up to her father for so long, she continually pushed her love for Scott deep down in her inner being. But the pain and sense of loss never completely vanished, and one day David ventured to ask her gently about Scott.

'Is there no chance you can sort out whatever it is that went wrong, Jo, dear? There are times, when you think no one is noticing that you look so . . .so sad.'

She looked at him, and felt the burning of unshed tears. 'I've never told you what happened to make me leave my job in Sydney, did I, Jimmy?'

They were sitting in a sheltered part of the garden, where an outdoor table and reclining chairs had been set up. Ann was inside catching up on some sewing for Angie as best she could. Her arm was healing well, and she was fully weight-bearing now, except after being on her feet too long. David would be back at work soon also, an occasional headache and backache his only legacy from the accident.

David frowned. 'Father rattled off some nonsense about what a dreadful nurse you'd turned out to be. I knew that was his vindictiveness showing again, so I didn't take any notice of it.' He stopped, and leaned forward. 'Don't tell me whatever happened has anything to do with Scott?'

'Not. . .not directly. But——' she bit her lip, and looked sadly at him '—it was after I told Scott something that happened in Africa that he went out of my life.'

She had become very close to David during the past weeks. Jodi's suggestion that she move out into a place of her own, had been greeted with such genuine dismay that she had let them talk her out of it.

They had previously talked with regret about the years they had grown apart. He had been absolutely furious with their father, once she had told him of the extent of his persistence in deriding her nursing skills, and his attempts to get her to study medicine. Both had agreed he was not rational about it, and wondered if something could have happened in the past to trigger off his obsession.

Now Jodi knew she needed to tell David all that had happened. The words began to spill out of her. She told him about Martin, and about the patient who had died.

And she even found herself telling him a little about the horror of the AIDS epidemic in Africa. It had been rife in their camp and surrounding villages. They had been able to diagnose a large number, and in the earlier months a good education programme had been started to try and stem its spread.

All of the people working in the hospital had also been heavily drilled in protective measures, not only to protect its spread through the health system, but so that the health workers themselves would not be at risk.

Then she told him about the horror of starving

people, people without hope. Sometimes people had just lain down in the streets outside the hospital and died, usually after surviving for weeks on the bush tracks, dodging guerrillas and walking for many, many miles without food.

'Oh, we managed to save quite a few. International aid did reach us,' she continued in a harsh, strained voice, 'but the streams of people just kept coming. Our supplies were basic at the best of times, but that last month the fighting over the border had escalated. There was no way we could cope with the influx of people. Quite a few of our earlier patients who had survived were very loyal to us. And the local health workers were marvellous. I. . .I was particularly fond of a young man called Danny. He always seemed to have a smile. He. . .he. . .'

David stopped her with a gentle hand on her arm. Only then did she realise that tears were streaming down her face.

'There was a news report about the raid on the hospital,' he said with emotion. 'It was on the news when we were on holidays. I realised it was the same address as yours and. . .and that's why we came home earlier than we had intended.'

Jodi stared at him in horror.

'We couldn't find out anything way up north, and I had to know you were all right,' he continued softly.

'So that's how Scott knew!' she burst out, and then she was pouring out the rest.

How there had been more than one raid the last week. How at first the hospital had not been touched, although a couple of times it had been caught in crossfire. Several of their friends and helpers had been shot.

Even women and children had not escaped. Sometimes she had thought the whimpering of seriously injured, dazed children had been the worst, but then there had been the helpless agony in their parent's eyes. The small medical team had worked day and night helping the wounded, doing what they could—which at times had seemed pitifully little.

Then there had been that last horrific raid. Only the arrival of the government soldiers, just in time, had prevented all of them from being killed.

'And the boy you were so fond of? Danny, I think you said his name was,' David asked in a murmur as Jodi paused, drained and dry in the mouth. 'What happened to him?'

'He. . .he was shot in that last raid,' Jodi whispered. 'The bullet lodged in an artery, and when we tried to take it out he. . .he. . .died.'

She couldn't continue. She couldn't tell him about that mistake she had made. Not now.

David was even more thoughtful and tender to Jodi in the days following her disclosures. She blossomed under the constant love and care that he and Ann showed her, and from the sheer relief of talking about the horror of it all. Scott had been so right. Angie just grew more adorable each day, and knew just how to twist her aunty around her little finger.

Jodi had not wanted to become any more involved with any of Scott's relatives, but had not been able to snub Liz who breezed in to see her several times. After one initial attempt to talk about Scott, she had given up as a tight-lipped Jodi had turned away.

On her last visit, she had tossed out the information that the family were all very pleased that Scott had at last bought into a general practice. Jodi had turned away again, although she had longed to know more about him. Liz had cut herself short and gone very quiet. Not long after, she had taken herself off.

After a cold few days to start with, the winter so far had been very mild, and by the middle of July many of the azaleas and other springtime blossoms had already started to flower. Jonquils had been flowering in sheltered areas for weeks, and soon the daffodils would unfold their long buds and lift their yellow trumpets towards the increasing warmth of the sun.

It was so different from the colder winters in Sydney, and Jodi marvelled at the early signs of spring, but she did succumb to a bad dose of flu. She spent a couple of days in bed, and when at last she was up and about she once again had lost weight. A hacking cough persisted, and when she at last insisted on going back to work she still had very little appetite.

'I'm sure you shouldn't be working yet,' a worried Ann said when she arrived home her first afternoon back. 'You're far too thin. I don't know what you're thinking of!'

It was lovely to have someone so concerned for her, and Jodi was compelled to agree with her there and then. But she felt better after a good night's sleep, and insisted on doing her rounds again.

She was still using the Land Rover, and when she pulled up outside Wingeen she was so weary she groaned when she saw a strange car there. Moreover, it was a bright red, latest-model Commodore Holden. The last thing she felt like was having to be sociable to the Wallaces' visitors.

It was only as she opened the front door to leave the keys for the Land Rover that it sank in that the number-plate on the Holden was yellow. It was registered in NSW.

There was a sound of heavy footsteps approaching, and as Jodi stood frozen Scott came into view.

'Hello, Jodi,' he said quietly. 'Edith just told me you were still with your brother.'

Her eyes feasted on his face. He looked paler and thinner than when she had seen him last. His eyes swept rapidly over her, and for a moment she thought she glimpsed something like anguish in his eyes.

'They. . .they didn't mention they were expecting you,' she managed to say, certain she must have been mistaken.

One eyebrow lifted. 'That's surprising,' he said curtly. 'Liz said she'd told you I'd bought into the practice here. Surely she told you I'd be back soon?'

'No. . .no. . .' she stammered. 'She did tell me you'd bought into a practice. I. . .I didn't dream it was this one. The. . .the patients will be glad. I. . . I. . .' Thoroughly confused, she held out the bunch of keys. 'Perhaps you'd give these to Edith for me?'

He took them, careful not to touch her. He stared at them, and then suddenly seemed to realise that she was in a white uniform. His expression hardened.

'And no one told me you were the new district nurse,' he said sharply. He paused, his gaze suddenly piercing. 'Aren't you taking rather a risk?'

She hardly heard him, only intent on getting away from him before she threw herself into his arms and begged him to love her. . .accept her. . .

She turned away without answering him, and started down the steps on her shaking legs. She was safely in David's car and had the motor running when she saw him suddenly start down the steps towards her. He was scowling ferociously at her.

What have I done now? she thought with a touch of panic. He must hate the thought that I'll be nursing his patients. She couldn't bear the thought that he despised her so much. He waved to her to stop, but she took off with some speed, leaving him staring after her.

She was only about a couple of kilometres away, when the tears were blinding her, and the sobs shaking her body so much that she pulled over to the side of the road. She didn't even move when she heard a car coming, nor when it stopped behind her.

Her door was pulled open violently. 'Jodi,' rasped Scott's voice, 'what's wrong?'

He almost lifted her from the car, and forced her face up so that he could see it. More sobs shook her helplessly.

'Oh, God,' he whispered, and it was a real prayer, 'you're so thin! Have you developed full-blown AIDS so quickly? Oh, why did I take so long to decide. . . to sell my house. I should have been here before!'

This time there was no mistaking the dreadful pain and anguish that twisted his face. Then, while she was still trying desperately to make sense of what he was saying, he crushed her against him.

'I'll look after you, my darling,' she heard him muttering into her hair in a desperate, driven voice. 'I won't let you suffer, and——'

'Scott. . . Scott. . .' she whispered in wonderment as she stopped crying. But he didn't seem to hear her, and she could feel the shudders that shook him.

'Scott!' She suddenly found the strength to push frantically against him until she was staring into his desperate, pain-filled eyes. 'What on earth are you raving on about?'

'I'm so sorry I left you before, Jodi,' he whispered. 'But I won't leave you again. I promise.'

There was no mistaking the love that glowed at her from his dark face. In a dream, she saw him lower his face, and then his lips were on hers, gently at first, and then that wild, hot surge swept through them, and they were straining against each other. His hands were suddenly inside her uniform, kneading her breasts almost painfully, and her bones melted in rapture.

Then suddenly a deep groan ripped through him, and he let her go. 'Dear heavens, that's why I left!' she heard him moan. 'I knew I wouldn't be able to stop making love to you. I love you so desperately!'

She gasped. 'I don't believe it. Did you just say you wouldn't be able to stop making love to me?' she said faintly.

He nodded jerkily, and she saw the look of disgust that crossed his pale face as he took a step back from her. Her heart nearly stopped, but then she saw clearly that he was not disgusted with her, but with himself!

'You. . .you really love me. . .' Her voice had grown stronger. Absolute bewilderment was starting to give way to a myriad emotions.

His hand came up and cradled her face. His fingers caressed the back of her neck behind her ears, and his thumb brushed at her wet cheek.

'I think I realised I loved you that second day I came home, and thought you had gone.' He smiled lovingly at her, and then his face distorted and he moved away again.

Jodi's heart was starting to lift. All this time he had loved her. All this time when she had been breaking her heart over him, he. . .he. . .

'You went away,' she blurted out, her voice rising, 'How could you go away like that if you loved me?'

'At first I don't think I knew what I was doing. Only a few hours before, I'd told your father I intended to marry you in the near future, as soon as I'd persuaded you to say yes. Then he'd have me to deal with. I was so shocked. All I knew was there was no future for us, Jodi. I couldn't risk you. . .you. . . You were already feeling so guilty because you'd already given someone AIDS, and——'

Sudden comprehension of what he was talking about swept through Jodi. And with it came a burst of anger. Pure, unadulterated anger swept through her in one almighty, cleansing wave.

'You think I've got AIDS?' she bellowed at him. 'All this time you've thought I was HIV positive! And now. . .now. . .I don't believe this!' Hardly aware of what she was saying, she flew at him, fists thumping into his chest in a frenzy. 'You stupid, stupid man! How could you? How dare you make such a mistake? Why didn't you ask me? Just four words would have done! *Are you HIV positive*. Just. . . Just four lousy words!'

Now it was Scott who looked first of all absolutely astounded, then filled with dawning comprehension, hope, and then wild, incredulous delight. It was as though he had stepped suddenly from the pit of hopelessness and death to the soaring mountains of heaven and life.

He opened his mouth to speak, but no words came out.

Jodi reached up to hold his face tightly, frantically, almost beside herself.

'It was a needle-stick injury! I was exhausted, as everyone was.' The words poured from her. 'Danny went to grab a tray just as I went to throw a used syringe into it. I knew the woman I'd just given the injection to was one of the people we had tested positive earlier that year, but I was careless. Three months later Danny tested positive, too!'

Hardly realising she was doing it, she shook Scott, desperate to tell him, to make him understand.

'Oh, I know *now* there's only a risk factor of four in a thousand being infected from a needle-stick injury. But I didn't then. And the mission director pointed out that no one could be sure where he picked up the virus. But, as you said, I was stressed out, burnt out, not thinking properly. And it was still something that should never have happened. And. . . I. . .I just felt so useless, so hopeless. . .so guilty. . .'

She shook him again, and then she was wrapped so tightly in his arms that she couldn't move, couldn't speak as his lips were on hers, swallowing her words into him.

She gave one quivering sob of sheer, utter delight, utter relief, and then she came alive in his arms. His hands and lips frantically left a trail of fire, as though he could not touch her enough, could still hardly believe she was safe in his arms at last.

She clung to him, her own hands holding him frantically, revelling in the solid feel of him against her.

He was in her arms. He loved her, and they had a lifetime together at last.

Well-remembered heat scorched through her, and she melted once again against him, no longer thinking coherently.

Jodi just knew that their love and passion for each

other blazed fiercely, and would continue to do so down through the years to come.

And so it proved to be. Not any of the ups and downs of a lifetime together ever succeeded in extinguishing the flame of their love.